DARK DREAMS OF THE ANCIENT ARCTIC

AJJIIT

SEAN A. TINSLEY
AND RACHEL A. QITSUALIK

ILLUSTRATED BY

ANDREW TRABBOLD

Published in Canada by Inhabit Media Inc. (www.inhabitmedia.com)

This book has been published with financial assistance from Canadian Heritage and the Department of Culture, Language, Elders and Youth (Government of Nunavut).

We acknowledge the support of the Canada Council for the Arts for our publishing program.

Canada Council   Conseil des Arts
for the Arts   du Canada

ISBN 978-1-926569-30-7

Printed in Canada
Library and Archives Canada Cataloguing in Publication

Tinsley, Sean A.
Ajjiit : dark dreams of the ancient Arctic / Sean A. Tinsley
and Rachel A. Qitsualik ; illustrated by Andrew Trabbold.

ISBN 978-1-926569-30-7

I. Qitsualik, Rachel A. II. Trabbold, Andrew III. Title.

PS8639.I597A35 2011   C813'.6   C2011-904241-X

Dedication

For John-John (1986–2008)

CONTENTS

INTRODUCTION 01

A NOTE ON LANGUAGE 05

ELDER 09

THE QALLUPILUQ FORGIVEN 45

OIL 57

THE FINAL CRAFT 67

THE MOON LORD'S CALL 81

THE WOLF WIGHT'S DIRGE 109

SLIPPERY BABIES 125

GHOST FLESH 139

DRUM'S SOUND 165

INTRODUCTION

We did not originally intend to provide an introduction with the collection of stories we call *Ajjiit*; though, as the work progressed, we thought it might be a good idea to offer some explanation for the admittedly peculiar content. There are always people who ask questions, for instance, wanting to know more about what an author might be alluding to when he or she births a particular phrase; and it eventually occurred to us that an introduction might serve as the opportunity to clarify our intent. So this is the "apology" (to use an old-fashioned term) for what we are writing, here. We cannot explain all, of course, since any fictional story is a bit like presenting theatre—everybody knows that it's not real mist creeping across the stage, but neither do we want to see the fellow off to the side, pumping out smoke.

Even the title gave us some problems. We easily agreed that the work should be called *Ajjiit*, but there was nail chewing over the subtitle (*Dark Dream of the Ancient Arctic*). Fantasy? Lore? Myth? Arctic? Inuit? We wanted to make it clear that we were not retelling any pre-existent Inuit stories; not playing the role of mythologists, but only writers. To a degree, our point, in crafting these fantasy stories, was to draw upon Inuit culture and lore, writing original fiction utilizing the unique creatures and concepts that Inuit once (and, in some cases, still do) fear or revere. Our main purpose, however, was to illustrate a sort of cosmological thinking particular to Inuit culture—a mystic tradition, if you will, that is not unlike the Arctic itself: barren to the superficial eye, yet filled with riches for those willing to fix a deep and non-judgemental stare.

There was a fine tradition of double, even triple, meanings in the ancient Inuktitut dialects, with references to a bubble (*pullaq, publaq*) as the soul, for example, since it is air (vitality or spirit) overlaid with a transient shell (the blood/flesh of the body). Such mystical allusions and euphemisms are simply further evidence of the genius of pre-colonial Inuit; evidence of minds whose connection to essential forces, such as the Land itself, have spawned high spiritual thought that some have even compared to Neoplatonic philosophy. Where possible, we have tried to do honour to this shamanic tradition, playing with our language to imply numinous powers, as pre-colonial Inuit stories and legends tended to do.

The idea, in ancient times, seemed to be that the tales needed to merge, conveying distinct mystical concepts only when they were viewed as a whole. This technique not only excluded listeners who were uninterested in, or flippant about, the relevant concepts, but also served to guard the specialized knowledge of the shamans by concealing it within common lore. Inuit have been called a "shy" folk, but it is probably more accurate to term them "elusive," for they traditionally dispel talk of their most sacred or horrific ideas with a smile and a joke. On the level of the bedtime story, then, the monsters and other fabulous beings of the Inuit imagination are but tools to thrill or put children to sleep. On the shaman's level, however, the *Unikkaaqtuat* (Ancient Tellings) discuss and access the Hidden world of the *Taissumani* (Long Ago), where the *Sivulivinit* (Ancient Ones) yet dwell in power and perpetuity. In this secret place, it might be best to view the superficially separate stories as one work.

Ajjiit, in the Inuktitut tongue of Inuit (Aivilingmiutaq dialect, most specifically), means "likenesses." It is an appropriate title, we think, because that was what we posed in our stories: likenesses of Inuit lore. Again, we did not rewrite traditional folktales, but instead created works of actual fantasy fiction utilizing the Arctic as a backdrop. In the way one might write a vampire story without making direct reference to past vampire works such as *Dracula*, so we borrowed concepts, monsters, and conventions from Inuit lore in order to tell our own tales. Some of the work (e.g., the *Igutaapiit* in "The Moon Lord's Call") was made up. Other parts of it (e.g., *Aagjuk* from "The Moon Lord's Call") were inspired by pre-existent myths and legends. One of the interesting features of Inuit stories is that they do not traditionally provide a lot of detail in their telling, so wherever we borrowed a pre-existent concept, we at once turned an eye toward those spaces where creativity might tramp and roar. Whether in enchasing fiery powers such as *Taqqiq*, or extruding foul creatures such as the *Qallupiluq*, we have had our fun. We make no promise to distinguish for a reader, herein. Some of this material, as one comes across it, might actually exist; while other features were born of tradition's flavour alone. However bright and solid it seems, we reflect, herein, but ancient dream.

— Rachel A. Qitsualik & Sean A. Tinsley

A NOTE
ON LANGUAGE

Out of respect for the Inuit culture, whose shamanism and unique cosmology has inspired our stories, we have tried to include as much archaic Inuktitut as is possible without (in our opinion) tripping up the narrative. Much of the Inuktitut terminology, where it occurs in the stories, derives from actually existent *sakausiit* (ancient songs of power) or *irinaliutit* (a sort of power-poetry); alternately, from the specialized vocabulary with which shamans were said to communicate with their unseen agents (a language known as *Tarriummak*).

Where possible, we have tried to avoid terms that possess traditional connotations within the English language, such as "spells," "magic," "spirits," etc. Such terms can do nothing but enfeeble the work, since Inuit once regarded exceptional or inhuman powers within the context of a distinct mindset, often viewing them as quite natural (rather than supernatural) phenomena permeating all of existence. Where we speak of the numinous in general, for example, one may note our preferred "Strength of the Land" (*Nunaup Sanngininga*), or such words as "Strength" or "Strong."

For those who prefer to consider language, our Inuktitut is mainly derived from the Iglulingmiutaq and Aivilingmiutaq dialects. In the interest of tidiness, Inuktitut words are italicized but once wherever they first occur in a story.

ELDER

"*Few are the Humble Folk,*" even one who knows the Land might say, "and strange. Who can understand, of them, but themselves?" But that same one might say that all folk are alike in some manner or other. It is perhaps only similarity that makes difference seem so monstrous. Here is a story of the Humble Folk, and especially, of one who differed.

o o o

Every awakening was like pain, and sleep delicious. Every hint of dream was to be cherished, as Pigliq had ever been a poor dreamer—a poor sleeper, kicking and crying out and awakening himself prematurely, in a way that was atypical for his kind. Among Pigliq's folk, dreaming was a skill, and many embraced the Grand Sleep with the same joy as expressed in those traditional games played after each waking.

It was the same pattern, every month: Pigliq and all his

kin felt the drowsiness steal upon them, knowing that it was time to finish only a few final tasks before the folding, the fading, the slumbering before arrival of newest moon. Such was the way of their sort of *Inugarulliit*. The giant folk, those who called themselves "Men" and "Women," and even "Children," called the Inugarulliit "Little Persons," but Pigliq's band of Inugarulliit knew themselves only as the Humble Folk.

Sometimes, when Pigliq thought about dreams long absent and past, he recalled some scraps about Men-and-Women—a towering folk who could not alter their size, as any one of the Humble Folk could. Male and female were the genders of these giants, as with Pigliq's folk, though they reproduced by strange means, coupling to produce young—the so-called Children—that grew like plants. Oddest of all, the Men-and-Women were one colour, coppery in skin tone. Men-and-Women made their clothes from animals as large as themselves, monster beasts such as caribou, as opposed to the lemmings that went into the clothes of the Humble Folk, and the caribou were worn with little or no alteration in their original hues.

At least, that was what Pigliq had heard. Pigliq had never seen a Man or Woman. He had only seen what they could accomplish, moving rocks as large as the ceiling over slumbering Inugarulliit heads; building great stone *inukshuk* columns toward their nebulous, gargantuan purposes. The Humble Folk disliked them for this reason. Men-and-Women were disturbers, almost the antithesis of the Inugarulliit, who wanted only to remain private and apart from the Land's larger life. Great animals such as caribou and white bears were dangerous, yes, but they at least did not overturn whole boulders in their quest for whatever drove the Men-and-Women giants.

It seemed Pigliq alone fancied that Men-and-Women were not as bad as Humble Folk traditionally depicted them. But then, he had a fondness for the Land's alternate sorts of life (such as the friend he called Haa, whom he had mentioned only to one other Inugarulliq). He had no practical basis for this fondness, other than the fact that he found his own kind tedious; nor had he often voiced his outlook, though he could see the questioning looks others gave him whenever he, unlike everyone else, failed to laugh as the storytellers entertained with tales of non-Inugarulliq monstrosity.

And as for the Men-and-Women, how could he dislike a strain of beings, however grotesque, who slept and awakened dozens of times before the arrival of each moon? The Men-and-Women, Pigliq supposed, were more like himself in this way. Pigliq was sick of being labelled *Tusaanngituq*—the "Never-listening One"—because he had difficulty in sleeping. It was assumed that he simply did not want to sleep, perhaps that he was defying the Great Sleep of the Humble Folk in order to prove that he was "special" (as some had come to mutter) and did not need the traditions of his kind. In truth, Pigliq had often sat under the light of past moons, weeping in frustration. He was not unlike the rest of his kind in the way of slumber's onset; and, in fact, hoped, with each new Sleep, that he would dream and awaken as easily as did his peers.

He never did.

He folded, faded, lost his colours like any one of the Humble Folk of time immemorial; he lost consciousness and rested like some ball of egg glaire upon the pile of lemming skins meant to provide his clothing for new awakening. But his dreams were weak, rarefied, like starveling shades of those grand imaginings owned by typical Humble Folk. The dreams of Pigliq's kind were supposed to be Strong, laced with that Strength which thrums through the Land's secret veins—a sweet decoction that had almost become alien to Pigliq: always, he neared the edge of waking consciousness while he slept (if "sleep" it could be called), so that his dreams never seemed to seize anything of their due Strength.

Monthly sleep had ever been the way of the Inugarulliit, Pigliq and his folk slumbering between the moons in their fullest;

but Pigliq, of late, seemed to be losing the skill.

It would not have been half the problem that it was, were it not for the fact that Pigliq also thrashed in his sleep, drawing his peers away from their own Strong dreaming. He was restless, it seemed, and not even that Strong insight of the Elders (honoured for wisdom, rather than age, for years meant nothing to the deathless Humble Folk) could come close to saying why. Thus had Pigliq been named with a word that made him wince whenever he heard it; for his name meant only:

"Bounce."

And his folk were stupid enough to believe that he had *chosen* this existence?

Such thoughts plagued Pigliq, slewing back and forth in his semi-conscious mind, as he fought to sleep—to dream.

To dream anything at all.

Even now, some part of Pigliq's mind tried to seize whatever wisps of dream danced just out of grasp, as this latest waking came on. It always seemed to go this way: Pigliq experienced his own uneasy form of the Grand Sleep, sheer length of time offering him just a bit more than superficial slumber; Stronger and *almost* actual dreams. And, in this way, he edged nearer and nearer to the Grand dreaming of any Inugarulliq . . .

But that was always when it was time to wake up.

New moon again, he thought—and that was that; as much as he tried to reject the invasion of wakeful thoughts, he was awake.

Pigliq almost immediately choked back a sob: the latest Grand Sleep was over, and he had dreamt nothing.

Pigliq swallowed, drew a great breath before sighing it out again, at once hearing the groans of those who had slept around him. His first sight was the light given off by the "pots," those fleshy cups sitting in incarnadine splendour at the centre of the cave he shared with a few others. The pots were almost a dozen, radiant and small and bucket-like, sown by the songs of Elders just before the Grand Sleep's full onset. As ever, the Elder-songs, strange and Strong, had been absorbed into the stone floor, into the deeps of the Land itself, germinating while all other Humble Folk (except Pigliq) dreamt. Now, the pots of Pigliq's particular chamber were ready and aglow, brimming with the Strong soot that would offer the awakened Humble Folk their new month's colours. The light of those pots shone about the cave, as though their relume were instead a song carried to the rich lichen sheathing walls and ceiling, caught by the lichen and sung back again with its returning glow.

Pigliq next saw his sleep-comrades (but one of whom he could any longer call friend) as their translucent, colourless forms shuddered, uncurling across their beds. Each bed had been a mere stack of lemming hides before the dreaming, from lemmings hunted and prepared before the Grand Sleep. Yet the Strong dreams of their owners had since moved deep in the Land's sinews, blurring matters of fact and fancy. The simple skin-piles were no longer beds, but had been transformed, so that they were now finished sets of clothes. Each of the Humble Folk awakened upon piled clothing: the pants, the inner and outer parkas, even the mitts and boots they would need in this moon's waking life.

All, that is, except Pigliq.

His dreams, more vanishing and wan than ever before, it seemed, had left him sprawled on a pile of old skins. Pigliq could not exactly see his limbs or body, since he was as yet uncoloured, but the hides had aged, between moons, beneath him. He could see bits of lemming hair clinging to his pellucid limbs, making them look as if they were afloat on water.

As ever, the loudest sounds of waking were those of laughter. The Humble Folk, when they caught sight of one another in translucency, greeted each other with chuckles that rose into lightsome, enthusiastic cries.

Pigliq watched six translucent blobs rise from their beds, don their clothes, a couple already moving toward the centre of the cave, even as he moved back. Unlike past awakenings, Pigliq did not pretend to laugh. His throat seemed bound with sinew, muted with shame.

"Don't sadden me, Pig," uttered a throat of velvet to Pigliq's right. The translucent form there, he knew, was a female and good friend. It was Mirsurti.

"I didn't do anything, Mir," Pigliq answered. Even to himself, the statement seemed defensive, as though he were defending his failed dreaming, rather than his current behaviour.

"Here," said Mirsurti, holding up a pair of pants. "I dreamt these for you, Pig."

"I'm not wearing your clothes, Mir," Pigliq muttered. It was a lame thing to say. He knew that Mirsurti's dreams were particularly Strong, even when interrupted by Pigliq thrashing about next to her. She had dreamt clothes for him, as well as her own, for the last several moons. Some disapproved of her for doing so, feeling that she was indulging Pigliq in his "attention-getting." Her clothes-making was how she had gained her latest name, which she seemed to bear in ignorance of the shame that, Pigliq thought, was implied by it:

"Seamstress."

"You're only going to colour your skin?" asked Mirsurti.

"No, I . . . think I'll go without," Pigliq answered.

"Without what? Colour?" said Mirsurti, sounding shocked. "At all?"

"Just this moon," Pigliq mumbled. "After all, nobody ever said I *need* colour."

Mirsurti fell silent, making Pigliq wish he could see her features. The possibility that he had injured her began to lure him out of his funk; he wanted to seem happy, even if it was just for her. His concern, however, arrived with a sudden, self-brutalizing wish: that he had never awakened at all.

Pigliq's lightless mood was utterly shattered when something struck the side of his head, wrenching a gasp from his throat. A greasy substance flowed down one cheek, his neck, and shoulder. Mirsurti let out a light cry, almost as startled as Pigliq himself, before streams of laughter emerged: the Humble Folk were already colouring one another with the soot of the pots—and someone had tossed a handful at Pigliq.

Pigliq, realizing that he was not going to escape the traditional chaos accompanying each colouring, begrudgingly accepted Mirsurti's clothes. By the time he was dressed, he even began to feel something of the Humble Folk nature take hold of him, for it had ever been the delight of the Inugarulliit to imbrue themselves in the Strong soot—a soot that brought new and random hues, rather than dark stains—beneath the new moon's call.

Pigliq found himself laughing, after that, scooping up his own handfuls to join in the riot of tincture. It was the eldritch festival, then—that which accompanied every wakening, with even the worst and weakest of dreams forgotten in a maelstrom of hue. As the Humble Folk hurled the offerings of their candescent pots, the Strength of the stuff clung to skin and hair and clothes, clung to being and reality, such that patterns stretched abloom across their forms. Pigliq's hair, worn loose and long to his waist, became visible with the polychromatic blush of his body. Mirsurti's high cheeks and dancing eyes, seeming to swim amid parti-coloured patterns, came into clarity. Qibjaaq, Siuk, Uriaq, Illuuq, Nasaq: all the others who had shared the chamber with Pigliq throughout the Grand Sleep. They emerged into full view, familiar as ever in shape, but newly made in the colours of wakening Strength. All, like Pigliq himself—like every one of the Humble Folk who had ever been—stood vibrant and aglow in saturation; with stipples that flashed like sun-bathed stones; with bands that streamed like exotic vapours; with whorls ablush like flowered trails. To the new moon's Strength, clothing and flesh were one, so that chroma crept as a dreaming oil into every stitch and strand of hair.

"Pig, your eyes are like night sky this time!" laughed Mirsurti.

"Yours are like blue coals," Pigliq said, "with little bits of gold." And they both laughed over the silliness of their own amusement.

Pigliq had almost forgotten his mood upon waking, when he turned at the sound of a male voice:

"My clothes aren't as well made," spat Uriaq. "Again. Better if someone hadn't distracted me from my dreams."

Uriaq stood with fists balled, staring at Pigliq. The temperamental Inugarulliq, who loved rendering his size larger than others, so that he now loomed over Pigliq, seemed to effloresce with varied purples, oranges, and greens. Uriaq's sentiment had already spread like some dark fire among the others, so that all laughter trailed off as he spoke. Mirsurti and Pigliq both stood wordless, casting nervous, sidelong glances at Uriaq. Pigliq himself hoped that it would not all end in a fight. He had only fought once, and the damage to the duelling cave had forced the Elders to declare a stalemate.

Uriaq stared at Pigliq, fists yet balled.

Worst part, Pigliq thought, *is he's right.* The fringed clothes of the Humble Folk were normally quite ornate, with male and female alike sporting patterns that brought to mind tumbling blossoms and sun-carven shadow. Uriaq, normally a very Strong dreamer (though no rival for Mirsurti), had awakened in clothes that could only be described as . . . well, boring.

They all had.

"I don't want to be in the same cave with you, anymore," spat Uriaq at Pigliq. "If you want to be stupid and not go to sleep, fine. But those of us who aren't freaks don't deserve to have our sleep disturbed."

Before Pigliq might have mumbled any apology, Mirsurti jumped to his defence (just as she had last moon), barking:

"It's up to you which cave you sleep in, Uriaq. If you don't like your new things, go sleep with the Elders, next. Try blaming *them* when you dream ugly clothes."

"Maybe I should blame them now," answered Uriaq, turning to Mirsurti, "since they ought to have done something about this Tusaanngituq here."

Begins again, Pigliq thought. *Here come the names.*

"We don't all have you to dream our clothes for us, Mir," added Siuk, a lithe female Inugarulliq who was never far behind Uriaq. She had once been a friend of Mirsurti's, though the two had had a falling out over pity for Pigliq.

As Pigliq expected, other voices grumbled in agreement. Inwardly, Pigliq's own was added to them. He wished that Mirsurti would just shut up, stop defending him, let him take his verbal beating.

"It's not like I'm dreaming really beautiful clothes," snapped Mirsurti at Siuk and Uriaq. "Not even for myself. Mine are just as—"

Mirsurti turned, shamefaced, to regard Pigliq. "Oh, Pig," she whispered, "I didn't mean to say you hurt my dreaming . . . ."

But you did anyway, Pigliq thought.

The moment of awkwardness was disrupted by a trailing cry, startling all. Every pair of eyes turned toward the source of the noise—toward the single entrance to the cave, a winding tunnel that led to the central nave of the Humble Folk home. Standing at that entrance was Nasaq, a short and normally shy male who liked to let a hood obscure overlarge eyes. Nasaq's form shone in twisting cinnabar and silver ticking, but Pigliq could instantly see that his breathing was fast, massive eyes wide and shining like saffron lamps beneath the edge of his hood. He looked mad. Before now, Pigliq had not even realized that Nasaq had left the chamber.

"The Elders!" cried Nasaq. And he disappeared around the corner, back into the tunnel.

Pigliq and Mirsurti frowned at each other, wondering what it was all about. Pigliq forgot about Uriaq and his complaints, until the large Inugarulliq shouldered past him.

Following Uriaq's lead, Pigliq and the four others left their

chamber, the glow of heavy lichen leading them in a double "S" through the tunnel's length, until they emerged into a much larger chamber: the centre of the Humble Folk home, which housed the Elders and those Strongest of Inugarulliit. There, Pigliq nearly crashed into Uriaq, who stood at the mouth of the chamber, wordless. Pigliq began to mutter something about the large Inugarulliq making a better wall than a doorway, until he, too, gazed into the chamber, falling silent with horror.

As with the chamber in which Pigliq had awakened, there were pots here, and they were many, rich and fat with Strength, illuming the chamber like so many tiny moons. But these pots were still full, brimming with the Strong soot of Elder dreaming, for no one had awakened to dip into them.

Nasaq was on his knees, now, in the very middle of the chamber, weeping aloud. He knelt amid the beds of the Elders— who were there, it seemed, but only in the strangest way.

Pigliq could *see* the Elders, though they were uncoloured. They were not translucent, watery in form, as the Humble Folk tended to be upon awakening. Instead, they were white, as blanched as old bone; as though the very stuff of them had become the opposite of what engorged the Strong pots. The Elders lay upon their beds—beds unchanged in the Grand Sleep, as with Pigliq's own, so that each was no more than a pile of old lemming skins. And the eyes of the Elders were closed in sleep. Their faces were twisted into expressions of sheerest horror, bleached countenances wracked as though yet in nightmare's grip. At first, Pigliq assumed that the Elders were moving slightly, albeit to strange rhythms. But he soon realized that they were stiff as lifeless carcasses under winter's wind. It was instead quite *other things* that moved about each of them, coiling like rings of black, of gold; things that snaked like oil upon running water; like dense smoke over whitened heads and rigid limbs.

Pigliq drifted into the chamber as though he himself were smoke, stunned and unbelieving of all he saw before him. For a moment, he even felt a strange twink of excitement, entertaining the idea:

What if wakening hasn't come? If it's a dream . . . ?

Yet Pigliq, whatever his peculiarities, was an Inugarulliq. He knew dream from reality, as others might know meat from stone, and here was a damp, grave, and waking truth. But what kind of truth was he gazing upon?

Pigliq heard Mirsurti, Uriaq, and the others, chattering in hushed and terror-strained voices behind him. He himself was terrified, even as he was fascinated. He neared one of the Elders, a female he recognized as caring little for him, though it was pitiable to see her rendered so, like some white ivory carving in the aspect, at once, of horror and repose. About her, the moving ringlets (parts that, Pigliq could now see, were joined together by cobwebby filaments) seemed to roil and caress the Elder, the smaller curls of black and gold staying close to her "flesh" (if it could yet be called that), while the oiliest thickness of the stuff branched out into larger whorls.

"Nasaq," Pigliq muttered, staring at the gold-and-ebon swirls, "did you find them like this?"

Nasaq provided no answer; and Pigliq would have turned to wonder why, but he had begun to see more as he stared into the larger rings branching out from the inky-gold stuff.

Pigliq's vision, it seemed, of a sudden *fell* into one of those rings, so that he saw events unfolding, enfolding him round. He saw himself in the ring, dancing with his fellow Inugarulliit under the new moon's silver. He saw snow kicked up underfoot—a powdery spray that momentarily obscured all but his own eyes, shining, and Mirsurti's eyes flashing under moon and star.

Then he saw the Land open beneath them, like a slashed belly.

He watched Mirsurti fall into darkness before he could catch her.

Pigliq watched himself run, along with other Humble

Folk, for the shelter of the caverns. He saw many of his folk make it before the Land opened yet again.

He heard their screams as the caves shut like snapping mouths upon all.

Pigliq staggered with the vision of himself staggering; fell to his knees with the vision of himself falling in the snow; felt his chin drawn upward with the sight of himself, horror-stricken, watching the pale moon descend like a great foot . . .

Pigliq fell backwards across the cold stone floor, gasping, scrambling until he was on his feet and well away from the black-and-gold horror that so hugged the Elder. He sensed, he *knew*, even as his vision was sundered from the thing's greater rings, that he had been attacked by a living thing. He could not say how or why. But he recognized it as he might his own name.

"Don't look at them!" Pigliq cried when he saw Mirsurti approaching another Elder.

"The Elders?" asked Mir. "Why? What's the matter with you, Pig?"

"Wants attention again," commented Uriaq, making no attempt to conceal the bile in his voice. "Always wants to be special."

Pigliq whirled in a semi-circle, of a sudden wracked with panic, addressing all who had awakened with him:

"Don't look at the smoke! The oil! Whatever it is! It's alive! Strong!"

Everyone, even Mirsurti, stood frowning at Pigliq, as though his very head had dropped off and rolled across the floor. For the moment, Pigliq didn't care. He was acting on impulse, yes, and making a grand fool of himself once again, but a sense of protectiveness had, of a sudden, caught him up as in a great gust.

They might think him mad at the moment, but at least his comrades had stopped moving toward the Elders.

"Nasaq!" Pigliq called, whirling when the corner of his vision caught sight of the small Inugarulliq yet kneeling, staring at a nearby Elder. "Nasaq, stop looking . . . "

But Pigliq's words withered between his teeth as he noted that Nasaq did not respond. The small Inugarulliq, the one who had alerted them all to what had befallen the Elders, sat staring. Nasaq's eyes, Pigliq realized, were upon one of the larger rings— enslaved to some vision of horror therein. Pigliq groaned, loathe to touch Nasaq, though he felt that there was no choice. He gave the hooded Inugarulliq a tap, a light touch on the shoulder, again calling his name. Then he pushed. Nasaq fell over on his side, hood open to reveal eyes wide and staring, as though still fixed on whatever the black-and-gold thing had offered.

Pigliq backed away, turned to fix his own eyes on the remaining Humble Folk, Mirsurti, Qibjaaq, Uriaq, and Siuk. All now stood atremble, like himself, voices stilled by terror.

"It's all!" cried a distant voice, that of Illuuq. Pigliq had not, until now, realized that she had been absent.

Illuuq's voice snapped everyone out of their panicked fugue, and they turned to see her standing at yet another mouth of the Elder-chamber. She spangled with the blue of beetle-shells, the jacinth of butterfly wings, but her face was anguished. Pigliq realized, after a moment, that Illuuq had been exploring the other sleep-chambers, of which there were five.

"All!" repeated Illuuq. "The only ones left are us!"

"Don't be stupid," spat Uriaq. But he then fell silent, and Pigliq suspected that the words had been hollow, born of the denial and fear they mutually shared. Pigliq could see the large Inugarulliq's fingers. Like his own, they trembled.

"But . . . have you looked in other chambers?" asked Mirsurti. Her normally soft voice was sharp, like shattered ice.

"All," repeated Illuuq. "All."

Pigliq's teeth ground together; he resented Illuuq for so hanging on that dread word:

All.

○ ○ ○

The Inugarulliit broke apart after that—at least, for a time. They spent unmeasured hours in roaming the tunnels, the chambers, checking and re-checking in a daze of confusion, of disbelief. None of them spoke. None met the eyes of the others as they passed, wandered, stood collecting themselves before beginning the mad cycle again. They were Inugarulliit; and despite personal differences, community was all they had ever known. Who would lead them to dance in honour of the newest moon? Who would organize the hunts, or declare which lemming-skins were fit for dreaming? Who would lace the Land with Grand Strength, in preparation for next month's Sleep? Who would administer the secrets, the precious mysteries of Inugarulliit life?

In time, the last six of the Humble Folk wandered back into the great chamber, where Elders lay fixed, whiter than quartz; where ebon and gold enwreathed; where Nasaq yet stared, enslaved by some alien flavour of horror; where visions at once bale and alluring promised from over every bed. Pigliq sat in a circle with the others, well away from the Elders and whatever the horrors were that held them, and joined the survivors in mute council.

There was some dazed wittering in time, during which someone perhaps inevitably asked:

"What could they be?"

No one answered. There were shrugs, some too-quick shakes of head. Everyone knew what the term "they" referred to.

"Destroyed," Qibjaaq at last mumbled. "The Elders. Destroyed." This Inugarulliq, silent till now, had turned out in vivid stripes with the colouring, but the same patterns now made his frown seem crooked. "Everyone's destroyed."

"No, they're not," spat Uriaq, casting Qibjaaq one of his more hateful looks.

"How do you know? They look—"

"They're NOT!"

Pigliq arose and left the circle. He could no longer stand the sound of Uriaq's trumpeting. Moving wide, he made his way past a few of the Elders (alive or dead, he himself could make no guess) until he stood by one of the tunnel mouths. There, he pressed his forehead into the lichen on the wall; its softness was a little thing, but any comfort was welcome.

"Pig?" came Mirsurti's voice.

She had followed him, and now stood near, though he didn't bother to turn and look at her. He sighed.

"Pig, do you think it's true?" asked Mirsurti. "The Elders, everyone else, they're not going to get better?"

"And how would I know?" Pigliq replied, voice muffled by the lichen.

Mir was silent for a long moment, before venturing:

"I just thought . . . I was wondering—could you ask Haa?"

Pigliq stiffened. "Ask him what?" he replied.

"Well, he knows things, doesn't he?" pressed Mirsurti. "You could ask him what's happening. What it means for us. Couldn't you?"

"He always demands a price," Pigliq said, turning to regard her.

"But he's your friend," said Mir. "Isn't he?"

"I don't know," Pigliq answered. "Yes, I guess, though we don't really think about each other that way. His folk, he says, always think about respect and trade."

"True friendship has nothing to do with trade, Pig," said Mirsurti. Her eyes seemed, of a sudden, hard.

"Even friends want favour for favour," Pigliq told her. In staring into the blue fires of her gaze, he almost added:

So what would you ask of me, when I owe you so much?

But Mirsurti met his stare, answering with speed:

"Loyalty to a friend is also to ourselves. Love has no parts."

And Pigliq gave her a wry smile, for he knew that she had guessed at his thoughts.

Hand in hand, Pigliq and Mirsurti walked back across the chamber, taking care not to stare into any of the rings afloat over the heads of the frozen Elders. Before they reached the others, who were yet sitting, Uriaq called out to them:

"I see he found another way to get attention!"

"Keep your mouth closed!" hollered Mir in return, letting go of Pigliq's hand. She used the same rainbow-dappled hand to point an accusing finger at Uriaq, then each of the others. "Pig has maybe saved all of us," continued Mirsurti. "Whatever those things are, they came after only the sleepers. Have you thought of that?"

"We were all sleeping," said Uriaq with some sourness.

"Not *well*," countered Mir. Then she frowned, turning to Pigliq.

"No offense," she told him.

Pigliq shrugged.

"Nasaq wasn't sleeping," Siuk argued.

"Something different happened to Nasaq," said Mirsurti. "He hasn't turned . . . white. And the . . . things aren't around him, like with the Elders. He's just staring."

Pigliq noted that there were no further responses, and the others seemed to be weighing Mirsurti's words. Perhaps they were even in agreement with her.

Am I? Pigliq wondered. He suspected that Mir was simply making things up in order to protect him. Again.

"You dream up good things for your pet Tusaanngituq here," spat Uriaq, waving a florescent hand in Pigliq's direction, "as well as you dream his clothes, Mir."

The arguing was renewed, then, reaching new heights, until nearly everyone was involved, though Pigliq soon tired of it. He drifted away, a step or two at a time, until the imperious voices of the Humble Folk sounded less jagged in his ears.

Would Haa know? Pigliq wondered. Perhaps Mir's idea wasn't a bad one. It had been some time since Pigliq had last spoken to Haa. Maybe it was time for a visit.

◦ ◦ ◦

Clutching a handful of lichen for illumination, Pigliq made his way down the secret passageway to Haa's chamber. As he walked, sometimes altering his size so as to squeeze past places where the tunnel walls pinched together, Pigliq poured his Strength—that which all Inugarulliit could wring from the Land to some extent—into the lichen he bore. As a result, it shed a flavescent glow caught up by the surrounding lichens of the tunnel walls, seeming to answer with their own light, as though in imitation. The result was that Pigliq could see every pore and striation of the stone around him. Yet as Pigliq wound his way ever downward, until the stone was slick and green, and the drip of water seemed to sound always out of sight, the light became wan: there was little lichen so far below and distant from the Elders, whose Strength had ever fed it.

In time, Pigliq could barely see by what he held in hand. He slipped often, trying not to curse aloud while sliding, on his back, along short sections of tunnel (for there were things, in the Land's deeps, that thrived in blackest rock, listening throughout eternity, ever famished).

Pigliq had forgotten how far it was to what he liked to think of as Haa's chamber, so as the tunnel's sheen gave way to sudden, vaulting blackness, he realized with a start that he had arrived. It was not, he knew, Haa's home. Pigliq would never see Haa's domain, for it was in depths of waters that Haa himself had but ill-described. This cavern held only a small pool without bottom, whose lightless extent funnelled into an underwater tunnel through which Haa came and went.

Pigliq cast a glance back up the way from which he had

come, having doubts about this meeting. Haa was a friend, of a sort, but his folk were ever insistent upon trade, even when it came to favours. For as their kind liked to say:

"Where there is respect between equals, there is trade."

Pigliq sighed, gripping his lichen tight in fist as he ap-proached the pool's edge. There, he paused, casting starry gaze about until he found Haa's token. It was a tooth, slim and translucent and sharper than any pin, from Haa's own mouth. It was lighter than a feather in Pigliq's hand, though it was, in comparison to the height Pigliq had chosen for himself, akin to a long knife. Pigliq himself had wrenched it from his friend's lower jaw, at Haa's behest. Left by the pool in case Pigliq needed to call upon Haa, the tooth was (as Haa liked to say) one of their mutual "pledges."

The "pledge" kept by Haa, from Pigliq, was that stuff with which Pigliq paid his friend.

With the token in hand, Pigliq stared into the dark pool, recalling the *irinaliut*—the Strong song by which the token might call out to Haa. Like the sough of wind, Pigliq sang:

Adust I lay in wintering grasp,
As feeble as a stone's own whelp,
Whose able eyes refused the gleam,
Of wend neath fluid flowing glim.
O send of me unfathomed help,
To trust regardant, gaze held fast!

Pigliq's eyes fell upon the tooth as he sang. The feel of the token, in his palm, remained unchanged, though it seemed to him that each word of the irinaliut warped it, drained it of its colour, so that it became as a spout of water in his grasp. This oddness had occurred before, and Pigliq knew that it would pass (though he had dropped the tooth, in fear, when he'd first sung to it). It was but the Strength of the Land arising with the song Haa had given him, moving up through Pigliq himself, out into the tooth, and passing by the Land's weirder traces to the token's former owner.

When Pigliq next glanced at the token, it was again a slender tooth. He sat cross-legged after that, placing the tooth between himself and the pool.

He waited. For some time, he waited. Haa was never quick.

A splash marked Haa's arrival, and a drum-like voice, saying:

"You immerse yourself in dark, Pigliq. It suits you, somehow."

"I dropped my lichen, Haa," Pigliq answered, though he could not as yet see his friend. "No point in wasting Strength just to stare at walls while I wait."

Haa emitted noise like a great yawn, and it reverberated about the cavern. He then exerted some trifling twink of his own Strength, so that Pigliq saw his friend's outline, peering from the water, and aglow. The radiance of Haa's skin increased, so that after a moment, Pigliq could see the broad maw—wide enough to take down Pigliq, at his current size, in a gulp. He could see the globular brown eyes framing the sides of his friend's head. By the time he could spot the spines along Haa's back, the traces of fins branching out to churn dark water, patterns of opaline light had come to wrestle between the dots across the Haa's skin, illuming the chamber and rendering the fish-being more beautiful than any *kanajuq* had ever been.

Or so Haa had told Pigliq. Pigliq had never seen another kanajuq fish; though he trusted Haa's authority on such things, when his friend described the creatures as the most cunning of water-breathers, able to make themselves indistinguishable from pebbles and river-bottoms at will. Haa had once mentioned that his admiration for them was the reason why, long ago, he had chosen the kanajuq's form for himself. Pigliq didn't really under-

stand what Haa meant when he went on about "choosing" forms, but he supposed that it was the usual way in which the Animal Folk thought: they, like the Men-and-Women giants, had almost no traffic with the Humble Folk; yet all of Pigliq's kind knew the Animal Folk to be grand with the Land's Strength, loving their play with shapes resembling bird, beast, and fish.

With Haa now glowing and visible, Pigliq arose from his sitting position and approached the very edge of the pool. There followed a short silence, before Haa said:

"The stuff of you is weightier than any stone around us, today. Have you come, Pigliq, to speak of something so serious? So unalike to the Humble Folk."

"You know," Pigliq answered with a smile that was almost a grimace, "I'm unlike the others."

"As yet unable to sleep properly?" Haa asked, some hint of pity in his tone. "To dream? Are you here to talk on that again? I am afraid I have no better answers than last time . . . "

"That's not why I'm here," Pigliq said. "A friend of mine, she had the idea to call you."

"You mentioned me to someone else?" Haa asked, bobbing slightly in the water. "Is that a good idea? Your Elders might not approve of you consorting with one such as myself. The Humble Folk make no sense but to themselves. Regardless, I comprehend that they are private."

Pigliq shook his head. "No, no, I mean, you're right," he said. "But the Elders never knew about you. Mirsurti . . . I only told her, and I trust her. She's the only one who's helped me. Or tried. She asked me to ask you about something. Something terrible, Haa."

"I do not serve the Humble Folk," the kanajuq-being said, batting great brown eyes. "I come to you alone, Pigliq. You alone saved me on that day when you found me here, far from the *Sanavik*, broken under the *Ijiraq* with which I had struggled. It was only because of you that I did not succumb to chimerism, depleted of the *innua* that might sustain my chosen *soma* . . .

As usual, Haa spoke of his Animal Folk mysticism as though it were readily comprehensible to Pigliq. As always, Pigliq listened politely, understanding nothing of which the kanajuq-being spoke, except for mention of "innua"—for this was what Pigliq had always paid out to Haa in return for his knowledge. It would be paid yet again, assuming Haa could help him.

"I'm asking for myself, too," Pigliq said, once the kanajuq-being let him get a word in edgewise. "Something has happened, Haa. Everyone . . . I mean, everyone and myself, awoke from our latest Sleep. Or, I mean, not everyone awoke. Only the ones that weren't . . . I don't know."

In stumbling words, as though he were describing a mad fantasy or warped dream, something to doubt and fear in wakeful telling, Pigliq took his time in relating to Haa what he knew—even simply guessed—of the horrors as they had played out since waking. The kanajuq-being did not speak while Pigliq told his tale, since this was the polite way of hearing a story amongst nearly all the Land's beings, but Haa registered either surprise or interest with a number of odd noises. The most interesting of all was the long, drawn-out groan the kanajuq-being made upon hearing of the oil-smoke oddities, gold-and-ebon, that curled about the whitened Elders.

When Pigliq had finished, silence fell about the chamber for a long moment, before Haa remarked:

"So. They are here."

Pigliq was taken aback. "What are here, Haa? The . . . smoke-things? You know them?"

"I have never seen one," Haa answered. "I know, rather, what they are. The beings that hold your Elders in thrall, Pigliq, arose from my own domain. From the sea's blackest parts. There are those, down there, who simply call them the *Sinnaktuumait*— 'Nightmares.' My own kind, the Animal Folk, know them of old as 'Dream Beggars.' Everyone likes to pick over terms."

"The sea?" Pigliq muttered. "Are you sure? The Humble Folk have nothing to do with that world." In merely thinking about the open waters, Pigliq experienced the normal Inugarulliq reaction of a shudder. The Humble Folk had always lived along the coasts, but without interacting with those beings who dwelt in the wet places. To Pigliq's knowledge, he alone had come to know one such being. But it was only because he was the Tusaanngituq: the one who had never listened to the Elders, and had explored the lower tunnels the Humble Folk so dreaded. It was here that he had first found Haa, heaving and pained and as close to destruction as one of the Animal Folk could get.

"As I said," the kanajuq-being corrected, "the Sinnaktuumait *arose* from my world. We were all wondering, to a greater or lesser degree, where they would shelter themselves now that they survive only on the surface. Some of the Animal Folk are actually hunting them. Not my set, though. Wise. Best not to get embrangled in such things."

"But . . . why here?" Pigliq asked. "Why didn't they stay in the sea?"

Haa seemed to think for a moment, before explaining:

"There has been a war, down below, of a kind. A harrowing, in the Deep Mother's realm. The hosts of She Down There finally expelled the Dream Beggars for all time. Such abominations are normally beneath Her notice. But they grew too fast. They spread too widely. These things cause imbalances. When they drew Her notice, and the Grand Eye opened—"

"Please, Haa," begged Pigliq, "just say why they're here! How are my friends, how am *I* going to survive, now they've destroyed the Elders? Now they've destroyed all but six of us?" Pigliq found himself nearly in tears as he spoke. Up till now, he had thought of himself as relatively uncaring. He had not before realized just how traumatic the situation was for him.

"Destroyed?" Haa replied. "Again, not listening. When did I say anything about destroying? I said they hold your Elders in thrall, Pigliq. Your other folk, too. It's what the Dream Beggars do. If they went around killing all the time, they wouldn't have a chance to eat. So to speak. And what they 'eat' are the Strong dreams of those they hold prisoner. No doubt, it's the dreaming that attracted them to your kith and kin. They'd have hungered after having been driven from the deeps. I dare say they may have found your folk through this very passage by which I visit you. No wonder the Humble Folk have nothing to do with the sea, with that kind of luck following them around."

Pigliq had fallen to a sitting position on the ground, head in hands. After a moment, he said:

"Destroyed or captured, Haa. It's the same. Without the Elders, there can be no Grand Sleep. No new cycles. No new dances under new moons. No Humble Folk."

Pigliq wasn't sure why he was so certain of such things. Perhaps it was simply that, increasingly, he was becoming teth-ered to despair. His world, of a sudden, seemed made wholly of fatigue. Of sadness. But some part of him at least thought:

Maybe it no longer matters if I can't dream . . .

"Nonsense," Haa responded with a disapproving burble. "The Elders must have come from *somewhere*. Else all Inugarulliit across the Land would go extinct with each little disaster. Perhaps this was meant to be, Pigliq. Perhaps you and your friends, strange as it seems, are now the new Elders. In a way." The kanajuq-being capped off his words with a wet chortle.

"I don't feel very Elderly," Pigliq muttered.

"Try to see the better side of things," Haa told him. "If you had not been owned of your sleep problem, you of certain would be unable to discuss all this with me."

Pigliq raised his head, looking questioningly at Haa.

"The Sinnaktuumait," Haa went on, "are drawn to dreams. Strong dreaming maddens them with hunger. If you are here to contemplate this, Pigliq, and not in their thrall, it is be-cause you were unable to dream. If you interfered with the dreaming of those near you during the Grand Sleep, it is possible that you may have kept them from the Dream Beggars. You may have done your friends a great service. The Land is strange. Perhaps it was meant to be."

A *service?* Pigliq wondered. Could that be true? Had his inability to sleep or dream actually meant some good? Of a sudden, he recalled Mirsurti's words to Uriaq and the others:

"*Pig has maybe saved all of us.*"

No, Pigliq thought, smothering his own hopes with savage insistence. *Nothing good about not sleeping. Nothing.*

He refused to believe that being a freak could be a good thing. He and the others, during the Grand Sleep, had simply been located in a cave too far away for the Sinnaktuumait to notice. That was all. The Dream Beggars had been too busy with the Elders, with the other Humble Folk more readily available, to go after Pigliq and comrades.

In fact, one of the Sinnaktuumait had almost caught Pigliq, hadn't it? When Pigliq had stared into one of its greater whorls, the visions therein had snatched at his mind, before he'd pulled away. That proved, to Pigliq, that he was far from immune to a Dream Beggar's powers.

"But," Pigliq asked Haa after a moment, "what happened to Nasaq? He wasn't dreaming when the . . . Dream Beggar caught him. And one almost caught me, too."

"Through the visions it showed you," Haa said, bobbing in the water as though to nod. "It's the way of the Sinnaktuumait with the wakened. You don't have to be asleep to have something like dreams, do you? Has your mind never floated adrift, especially when weary? So that you might as well be asleep? This weaker strain of dreaming, too, the Sinnaktuumait can feed upon. But they need to fortify it. To Strengthen it. And they do this by immuring the mind in horror. It is their preferred way. Their kind of predation. My set once captured one for study. It was concluded that terror begets the Strongest kind of dreams. And, other than destroying the Sinnaktuumait, which even the great Agonies find difficult, there seems to be no way of liberating minds so enslaved to such dreaming . . . "

Pigliq climbed to his feet, rigid, staring. He was oblivious to much of Haa's mystic rambling, but his mind fixed itself on those two words: "dreams" and "dreaming."

"So, the waking visions," Pigliq interrupted. "Like whatever Nasaq's caught up in—they're actual dreams?"

"Of certain, yes," Haa replied, sounding puzzled.

"I have to go," Pigliq mumbled.

"But . . . this instant?" the kanajuq-being asked. Then, perhaps guessing at Pigliq's thoughts, Haa asked:

"Would you risk the nightmares of the Sinnaktuumait? For some paltry chance to dream, Pigliq?"

"Not paltry!" Pigliq insisted, his voice—his *mind*—harder than the stone around him. "Not to me and mine. I'll never really understand you, Haa. I'm not one of the Animal Folk. But you can't understand me, either."

"I'm not one of the Humble Folk," Haa said after a moment. "But things are as they are. And this means I may never hear a call from you again, Pigliq."

"Yes," Pigliq said.

"There are few beings that I would miss, Inugarulliq," said the kanajuq-being. "But I will miss you. You, I would call equal. Perhaps friend."

"Yes," Pigliq said.

"And where there is respect, among equals," Haa said, invoking the ancient expression of the Animal Folk;

"—there is trade," Pigliq finished.

o o o

Pigliq raced up the winding tunnel with all the speed he could muster, knees and wrists already battered from slipping numerous times. Over much of the distance, he was weary, and he could not recall his own name. Such had ever been the effects of giving innua, the stuff Haa needed in return for his wisdom; that subtle vapour lending the mind its thoughts of "I," the heart its feelings of "we." Or so Haa had always claimed. In the past, the kanajuq-being had tried to explain the role of innua as one of the threefold elements of existence, insisting that sentience was impossible without it. Pigliq, uninterested, had barely absorbed this much. He knew only that, after the loss of this so-called innua, he was scatter-brained, as though some Hidden pillar, supporting ego, had been made to shiver and wobble.

Now, Pigliq's mind was feverish with purpose, and this impelled him like some coloured sling-stone up the passageway despite his fatigue. His full sense of memory, identity, was with him again by the time he reached the chamber of the Elders.

The first being Pigliq saw was Uriaq, looming and ugly of aspect, despite the swag of his colouring. The large Inugarulliq spotted Pigliq as he emerged from the tunnel, spitting out:

"There's the Tusaanngituq! Have fun, playing in your tunnels, while we're trying to figure out what to do?"

As Pigliq made to move around him, Uriaq caught him by the arm, adding:

"Mir thought maybe one those smoke-things got you. I said, if they did, at least we'd be able to sleep from now on—"

"Don't touch me," Pigliq muttered, looking up into Uriaq's empurpled eyes. While he did so, the Strength within him welled, perhaps spurred by anger at being delayed from his purpose, and it manifested as silvern tendrils that spiralled, creeping and barbed, up Uriaq's forearm.

Uriaq pulled his arm back, shaking off the manifestation of Pigliq's Strength, his patterned face displaying scandal. "We're not allowed to duel," the large Inugarulliq whinged. "No Elders to oversee it." He took up a stance well away from Pigliq, as though the latter were toxic.

"Don't touch me," Pigliq said, and moved deeper into the room.

Before Pigliq could draw near enough to one of the Elders—all still whitened, still rigid on their beds—to see any particular vision offered by the Sinnaktuumait, Mirsurti blocked his path.

"Pig!" she cried. "Where are you going?" Then, leaning close and adopting a hushed tone, she asked:

"Have you seen Haa?"

Pigliq's first reaction, rather than to greet her, was to narrow his eyes in irritation. Then, sucking in a deep breath to fuel some bit of patience, he met her gaze. His intention was to tell her, in level and geometrical terms, that he had ever been an outsider, ever stood apart from the Humble Folk, albeit through no choice of his own. There was no justice, he had reasoned, in preventing him from making his own choices now, when he had never enjoyed the benefits of harmony with his society.

But when he saw the concern, the care, in Mirsurti's orbs of gold-flecked azure, something in him softened.

"Thank-you," Pigliq told her. "Thank-you, Mir."

"Pig, you're frightening me," Mirsurti said. "Did something go wrong with Haa? Why are you just walking over to those . . . "

"Sinnaktuumait," Pigliq finished for her. "Dream Beggars. I need to see them, Mir. Goodbye."

Mirsurti's eyes widened in panic. Moving, keeping her hands on Pigliq all the while, she came to stand directly in front of him, as though to keep his view from the Sinnaktuumait.

"What has Haa done to you?" she asked, no longer keeping her voice down. "Is Haa making you like this? I should never have told you to see him!"

"It's all well," Pigliq said with a smile. Perhaps there was the slightest chance that he could make her understand. "They'll make me dream, Mir. That's what they do. You and the others should move off, now. Find a new place. You're Strong. Maybe you can find out how to replace—"

"No," interrupted Mirsurti, shaking her head. "You're speaking like you're locked in nightmare."

Pigliq almost laughed. "Not yet," he said. "Soon. At least it's a kind of dream—"

Pigliq's next moment of awareness came with the realization that he was lying on the smooth stone of the cavern floor, eyes playing across patches of lichen aglow upon the domed ceiling. Of a sudden, he remembered the hardness of Mirsurti's eyes, as though they had become twin glacial shards, before the Strength had exploded from her. It had flashed like the glimpse of some colossal blossom, petals of every colour snapping in upon Pigliq. It had hurled him back and down, stunning and leaving him to remember why he was on his back.

Before Pigliq could recover, Mirsurti sat on his chest, pinning him to the floor. The hardness was yet there, in her eyes, Strength snaking like blue roots from the corners, readying to emerge again. Pigliq wondered if he might survive another strike.

"You can't duel!" a voice cried. It might have been Siuk's or Illuuq's. It was soon after joined by Qibjaaq, crying, "There are no Elders to judge it!"

Mirsurti neither looked away from Pigliq, nor addressed anyone but Pigliq himself:

"I don't know what Haa has done to you. But I'm not letting you destroy yourself."

Pigliq tried to answer, but he merely choked, beginning to sob.

She doesn't understand, he thought. *No one understands. They all dream.*

When Mirsurti saw the tears streaming from each corner of Pigliq's face, her visage became one of mingled horror and pity. Slowly, she rose to her feet, helping Pigliq up from the floor. By the time Pigliq was on his feet, his weeping was open and unrestrained.

"Pig, what has happened to you?" whispered Mirsurti.

"You'll never know," Pigliq answered between sobs. "You dream. Every time. You don't know what it's like not to dream."

Mirsurti made no answer, but only stared for a long moment. Then she nodded, and the Strength in her eyes withdrew. Of a sudden, she looked more tired, more sad, than Pigliq had ever seen her.

The remaining Humble Folk stood still and silent in the cavern of the Elders, as frozen as the imprisoned Elders themselves, so that the only movements were the continued coiling and roiling of the Dream Beggars. In time, Uriaq turned and walked back down the tunnel that led to their original sleeping chamber, but to what purpose, Pigliq neither knew nor cared. Within seconds, the others followed—all except Mirsurti, who stared at the chamber floor, the Strength of her eyes replaced by tears.

Pigliq approached Mirsurti long enough to leave the lightest of kisses on one dappled cheek, before he chose a single Dream Beggar. Mirsurti made no response as he turned from her.

The Dream Beggar seemed to grow more active in its roiling as Pigliq approached, as though it sensed his purpose. The black and gold of its coils tightened, played rapidly over the Elder it held like some ivory carving beneath it, and some strands of the creature stretched, circled high and apart from the rest of its substance. These married themselves into a great whorl, then a circle filled with vision as of starry skies, as though in greeting of Pigliq's regard.

Pigliq stopped, standing close to the thing.

Into its circle, he stared, unblinking.

Dream, he told himself, even as he shook with both fear and expectation.

Faster, much faster than before, Pigliq's awareness plunged into the pool of the Dream Beggar's vision. As before, he had the sense of this creature's life, its vital essence and Strength surrounding him, filling his perception with something like inverse light, and *need*—need every ounce as urgent as Pigliq's own to dream.

Then came the nightmares, visions of horror like spines to impale Pigliq's mind, pinning it to the phantom frame of the Dream Beggar itself. It prepared to drink of him, Pigliq sensed; to cut him upon itself, as though it had become a living blade clutching him close to breast, with its mind serving as the basin into which Pigliq's own mind would bleed.

Even with this realization, Pigliq felt no regret. It was not as the others had said: he *was* one of the Humble Folk—a true Inugarulliq, and craving of dream. Even if that dream was agony.

As Pigliq prepared for the Dream Beggar to impale him fully upon the lance of its mind, Pigliq regretted nothing—until he heard a voice in his ear:

"Loyalty to a friend is also to ourselves. I'm not going to let you be alone, Pig. Love has no parts."

Mirsurti.

Of a sudden, like a gasp of air before diving, Pigliq managed to regain some sense of his body; of something apart from his nightmare-enwreathed mind. He sensed Mirsurti, standing behind him, a gentle hand on each of his upper arms. He sensed the sharpness of her jaw as it rested on his left shoulder. He sensed her ear cupped against his own, and he knew.

She, too, was staring into the Dream Beggar's vision. The same vision.

She was trying to climb into the nightmare with him.

Pigliq struggled, then, though not bodily. His last awareness of the physical, of the real, had been as fleeting as the spangle of snow in moonlight, and the grip of the Dream Beggar encircled like a tarry surge about him. His mind was swept up on it, each independent thought smothered as it struggled to be born within his consciousness. Still, Pigliq fought to think at all, to focus on something other than whatever visions the Dream Beggar pressed into his perception. From the outset, he invested his personal Strength—not inconsiderable—into the battle, only to find it poured out of him like water from a simple jug. He had remaining, after that, only one great terror—a horror far greater than anything any Dream Beggar might offer him, and this he wielded as his lone weapon. This was the horror of knowing Mirsurti enslaved, her beauty and power degraded in the cess of this thing from the sea's bottom, a thing which possessed no dreams of its own, but which fed solely on the imaginings of others.

And Pigliq, of a sudden, refused to dream for this thing. He refused. So, with all the agony with which he had once wished to dream, with all the isolation and loneliness with which he had once raised sleep up as a thing commanding worship, he resisted.

And he became as a great vacuum within the mind of the Dream Beggar.

The void in which nothing dreamt, but in which Pigliq himself stood firm at centre, began to consume the Dream Beggar. The un-dreams enwreathed Pigliq, there, like a grand cloak of unknowable colour. And he felt the death of the Dream Beggar, thinned and screaming, its last wail devoured in anti-dream.

At the end, after time unknown, there was no sense of life other than Pigliq's own, in his mind, and he realized that the Dream Beggar was gone.

He blinked, becoming aware of the chamber of Elders once again, though the Dream Beggar whose visions he had indulged was no more.

Mirsurti squeezed Pigliq's hand then, and he looked down to see where she had collapsed at his left. She had fallen, her mind partly ravaged by the Dream Beggar's visions, though even as Pigliq had fought the abomination, her fingers had remained entwined with his own. Here, Pigliq realized, as tears welled in his eyes, was a Strength far beyond that of the Land.

Pigliq helped Mirsurti to her feet, embracing her with care, as though she might crumble before him; and she smiled, her eyes yet aglow with azure.

Then the two of them noticed the Elder, a male Inugarulliq

no longer enslaved to the Dream Beggar, the whiteness retreating from over his body like thinnest frost beneath sun. The Elder looked up at them as might some fledgling bird, as uncoloured as newly formed ice, and apparently dazed.

"Thank-you," the Elder whispered.

Mirsurti drew in a sharp breath, pointing about the chamber, to where the Sinnaktuumait were streaming away from all their captives, like smoke of ebon and gold caught up in strange winds. As Pigliq watched, their oily tendrils spiralled together near the centre of the chamber, to be joined by Dream Beggars swirling in from adjacent chambers. Once together, it was impossible to tell one from another. The great mass of them seemed to decide, for a moment, on which direction in which they might all swirl. Then they raced, like a gold-and-ebon storm, down the passageway to Haa's pool.

Back to sea, Pigliq thought.

Along with Pigliq, Mirsurti watched the Sinnaktuumait flee, and she whispered near his ear:

"They fear you now."

It was a strange new time, for Pigliq, after that. The Elders were again awake, and with little ceremony they coloured themselves before taking Pigliq and the others aside, to discuss all that had transpired. There was a peculiar scent of the Strength about Pigliq, now, and all of his former peers, except for Mirsurti, fell mute about him—as though they were at once in awe and fear of whatever had touched upon him.

Before the new moon's dance, Pigliq alone held council with the Elders. They treated him in an odd way, at that time, and it took Pigliq some effort to realize that they were treating him as one of their own number. And it was true, as it turned out, that Pigliq was now an Elder, for as the former Elders explained, the Strength of dreams was the discipline of dreams, and only the control of dream, as Pigliq had now gained, was what wrought an Elder from one of the common Humble Folk.

It was also explained, however, that Pigliq could not stay among the Humble Folk. Here, he learned, was the great secret of how the Inugarulliit perpetuated themselves: it was the custom that, in those rare instances when new Elders arose, they were to leave the caves of the Humble Folk under moonlight, braving the hazards of the open Land to seek others such as themselves. If all were Strong enough, and strong enough, they would together found a new home.

o o o

And if one were to ask one such as Haa whatever became of that Inugarulliq who had been named Pigliq, he might answer (but at a price):

"Taking a different name, that new Elder left his old life. He took with him the one he loved, once called Mirsurti, and they departed in moonbeam and happiness. Their time was not easy. For the Land never meant it so for any life. But they met others like themselves. And the paths of the Land brought them, in time, to a place in the living rock. And they founded there a Strong dwelling, and made it joyful. And they came, there, to discover that other secret, which is the one of making more alike to themselves. Why all the secrets, no one knows. These are the Humble Folk, and who but themselves can understand?"

THE QALLUPILUQ FORGIVEN

Burning cold in the sky, the moon was round and full when the Qallupiluq emerged from the sea.

Bathed in silver light, the Qallupiluq hauled itself onto to the ice at the water's edge, squatting among the pressure ridges that wound like shattered labyrinths along the shoreline. The chimera's spines shed droplets of brine, shivering in the winter air—but never with cold, for the Qallupiluq knew nothing of temperature. Instead, the Qallupiluq shook as might a man or woman in the throes of disturbed slumber. In truth, the chimera was dreaming, and its dreams were of that which it had never naturally possessed: *form*.

The Qallupiluq detested the very feel of form, since shape meant discipline, and discipline meant control. Of all the *inuunng-ittut* (non-Human beings), the Qallupiluq's kind most despised anything that threatened to burden them with the shackles of order. But this Qallupiluq knew that it was out of the water's sheltering darkness, and now on the open *Nuna*. There were different laws upon this, the Land; and of all domains, the Land demanded discipline.

So, the Qallupiluq forced upon itself a waking dream, the dream that promised change. And the form the chimera dreamt was that of a Human, a girl that it had met many years ago. The dreamer pulled its seething flesh in tighter as it visualized her, a breeding age female who had broken taboo one day, combing her long and lovely hair by the edge of an ice-crack. The Qallupiluq had pulled her in, then, swimming deep with her—a foolish thing to do. Nothing but dead eyes had met the Qallupiluq's own in the gelid depths, the girl having either frozen or drowned to death before the slightest whiff of her life might be sampled. It was a fantasy of the Qallupiluq's, to but once have the merest taste of the life-breath; and it was a fantasy that danced ever out of reach. Mistakes did happen. The fragility of Human life, whatever trail upon which it made to and fro, was something that the Qallupiluq had never been able to fathom.

Now, the Qallupiluq dreamt, and it dreamt of *her* form. Such dreams were not entirely of the Human stuff, for these ran like roots into the veiled Land—that unseen Land which governs even the sea—where they drew upon timeless wells of Strength. Such Strong dreams came trickling upward, to roil like curdling milk in the Qallupiluq's hollow breast. There, the Strength was empoisoned with memories of hatred, with condemnation and wrath. There, the Strength of the Land reshaped the Qallupiluq, according to the latter's will, into the form of the long-dead girl. It seemed that the Qallupiluq was very still for a time, perhaps even asleep, and when the chimera again moved, it stood upon Human feet. A girl's dark eyes examined the smooth skin of a girl's amber hands, shortly before those same hands tugged at the hem of Human garments. The Qallupiluq saw raven hair at play in the wind, and the chimera shivered at the feel of those same locks affixed to its own head. The Qallupiluq knew that it was now fully clothed in Human form, in the dream of a girl who lived no longer. The chimera also knew that its mask was near-perfect, but for breath: there was no vapour in the moonlight, for the Qallupiluq's false lungs could do nothing to simulate the girl's *anirniq*—the life-breath that had been hers alone.

But how pretty I am, the Qallupiluq thought, and it laughed with the sound of sundered ice.

The final details had taken shape, and the Qallupiluq stood as a girl fully clothed in strange garments of fur and fawn. The Qallupiluq immediately shook its head (the girl's head), knowing that it was not remembering the clothing correctly. How could it, never having needed such things? But perhaps, in the gloom of winter, such rags might trick even Human eyes. The chimera paused, reaching one hand in back of it, to check for a hood: this, too, was ill-wrought, being vast and sacklike and more than a little lopsided. Still, it would have to do in the hours ahead.

The Qallupiluq turned inland, taking a moment to get its bearings, whereupon its girl's lips smiled. To the northeast, the chimera knew, was the camp. The Humans lived there, for they had settled near the coast that was the Qallupiluq's own. The Qallupiluq had endured them for less than a month, though every hour of their presence had seemed like a cycle of the moon. Even in the depths, the Qallupiluq had been assailed by their emotional stench—by hope, by love, by despicable joy. The stuff of their laughter had penetrated even the deep shadow, rasping at the Qallupiluq to the point of pain.

Yet these same Humans had given the Qallupiluq a gift, of a sort.

Three days ago, a pack of Humans had come down to the sea ice. Whatever they had been doing (catching fish, washing, or something altogether different: the Qallupiluq couldn't have cared less), they had made the mistake of allowing one of their spawn to play near an ice-crack. And while this child had sat singing to herself, the chimera had drawn near, listening from below, waiting for any little violation of taboo that might have allowed it to leap and seize the Human calf. No such violation had occurred—until the child had walked away. Even as the child had left the ice-crack, the Qallupiluq had felt a ripple in the Strength of the Land, hearing the child uttering the words:

"I wish I saw a Qallupiluq . . . "

Since the time of those foolish words, the ancient laws of taboo had lent the Qallupiluq the necessary Strength to seize that child. For three days, such Strength had gathered, and now—under this gravid moon—the chimera would seek out its prize.

As a girl, the Qallupiluq walked, and soon its legs were almost steady in the snow.

Little time elapsed before the camp was within sight, marked by the multiple domes of snow in which wintering Humans dwelt. Most, the Qallupiluq noticed, were aglow with the flames that Humans so carefully cultivated against the cold. Further, the chimera saw dark, boulder-like spheres at the edge of the camp, and knew that these were most likely dogs. The Qallupiluq was wary of them, even though the chimera feared neither tooth nor tip of spear. Instead, it was concerned that the beasts might raise an alarm. They might yet alert the rare ones among the Humans: those Some Seen, who possessed the power and knowledge to strike down even the Qallupiluq's kind.

Struggling to maintain the false form, the Qallupiluq raised its eyes to regard the *Aqsarniit*, whose emerald streams of light ever undulated across the dark dome of the sky. The Qallupiluq whistled then, airless, without sound or vapour, sending forth its intent like a lengthening shadow. The chimera's will stole softly across the Human camp, and with the sending went the power of sleep. By the time the Qallupiluq ceased to whistle, it knew that all creatures in that camp—including the wretched dogs—had fallen into deepest slumber.

The Qallupiluq could already smell the taboo violator, the

child who had wished to "see a Qallupiluq" by the ice-crack. The scent of transgression, more delicious than freshly spilt blood, indelibly marked the *iglu* in which the child slept. Now loping, not at all like the dead girl the chimera resembled, the Qallupiluq made its way there in great strides.

Finally standing by the snow-dome in which it was sure to find the child, the Qallupiluq paused. The chimera would not creep in like some penitent guest, but instead prepared itself to rend the dome asunder. The Qallupiluq spread its arms, gathering the Strength to do such, when it was startled by a voice:

"You have no breath."

The Qallupiluq was not only shocked by the fact that there was someone yet awake in the camp, but by the language in which the words had been spoken—for the statement had been in *Tarriummak*, that secret tongue which only the Strong inuunngit-tut and the Some Seen know.

The Qallupiluq wheeled, but saw only a dog. The canine, whose coat was coloured as of rusty rocks, sat watching the Qal-lupiluq with eyes of palest yellow. It sat on its haunches, neither threatening nor cowering, while the dogs around it slumbered.

"You have no breath of your own," the dog repeated, again in Tarriummak. Its pale eyes did not blink.

"What speaks to me," the Qallupiluq asked in the same tongue, "that resists my will?"

"A dog," the dog said.

"No dog," the Qallupiluq said, "but a liar. You possess Strength. You are Hidden."

"I am a dog," the dog said.

The Qallupiluq was silent for a time, while the wind made false locks dance about its head. Finally, the chimera said:

"Whatever you are, you will not interfere with my mis-sion."

"Mission?" the dog asked. The animal was perfectly still as it spoke, eyes unblinking, unwavering. "What mission brings a

Qallupiluq among Humanity?" it asked. "Have the depths grown too warm? Does the blood of seal and whale no longer offer sport?"

"Mock as you will, dog thing," the Qallupiluq answered, "but my mission is a sacred one. A cleansing one." Then the chimera pointed at the iglu next to it, adding, "Here is a Human calf who has violated taboo. I am authorized to act upon her. The Land demands it."

"Is it the Land's demand?" the dog asked. "Or your own?"

The Qallupiluq said nothing, but stood staring at the dog with hateful Human eyes.

"Consider the path you tread," the dog went on. "There is correct and incorrect behaviour—yes. But woe to the one who takes up the burden of executioner as though it were a gift. It is a little thing, the forgiveness that Humans practice amongst each other. But it has Strength above Strength."

The Qallupiluq laughed with the sound of splintering shale. "There is no Strength at all in little things, dog," the chimera said. "If we are to do battle, then come."

"I do not bring conflict," the dog said. "I bring you forgiveness."

Something seemed to well within the Qallupiluq, then, a poison the chimera barely understood, even as the sentiment blinded the Qallupiluq with the rage such emotion spawned. In response, empoisoned Strength spilled from the Qallupiluq, so that its fury nearly blew the adjacent iglu apart. Not pausing for a moment, the Qallupiluq leapt down into the sunken floor of the devastated home, invisible tendrils of sense reaching out. There was a Human family here, all stilled by the chimera's black will; still asleep among the bits of shattered snow-wall. The Human calves were many, male and female, and the Qallupiluq would not have been able to tell one from another, were it not for the distinct stench of a taboo violator. The fetor hovered over one girl-child no higher than a woman's waist. This one, the Qallupiluq plucked from her bed without hesitation, shuddering at the exotic scent of her life. With a physical strength far greater than that of the body the Qallupiluq currently imitated, the chimera took little effort to fit the slumbering girl into its vast hood.

With the taboo violator securely in place, the Qallupiluq leapt from the iglu, ready for imminent attack. But the dog, good as its word, was gone. The camp was utterly still. Such facts, rather than putting the Qallupiluq at ease, somehow agitated it all the more, making the chimera eager to regain the sea's embrace. So it ran, in great vaulting strides, as though its form were that of a colossus rather than a girl. The Qallupiluq ran with something akin to panic, accelerating as it went, for the chimera sensed something of ill omen in the way things had gone with the dog.

In the deep black, the Qallupiluq thought, *she's mine. Like the one whose skin I wear. Like the ones before her. As with all the taboo violators . . .*

Its mind awhirl with shadowed thoughts, the Qallupiluq's discipline began to erode, and, as the snowfall thickened, the Qallupiluq's run became something more like a shamble. By the time the brash of ice dividing the chimera's home from the Nuna came into sight, the Qallupiluq could see that its fingers were no longer distinct. The chimera's flesh had grown dark and piscine, stretched across spinous fins like those of the *kanajuq*, or sculpin fish. No matter. The Qallupiluq alternately scrambled and picked its way past the pressure ridges, until patience at last saw it to the water of an ice-crack.

The Qallupiluq placed one fin-like foot into the ice-crack's water, before it was startled by the cry of the child in its hood. The Qallupiluq grinned a lipless grin, then, at first certain that the taboo violator had awakened, and now understood the doom before her.

But the child was not truly crying.

She was singing.

In the language of Tarriummak.

And the water was gone.

The Qallupiluq cried out, discovering that its foot had become locked into an ice-crack that no longer existed—for the song of the child upon its back had frozen the water solid. The Qallupiluq then felt the tiny hands of the same child, twin fluttering touches, as their palms came against the chimera's skin. And at the touch of the child, an azure flame seemed to erupt from the Qallupiluq's hood, its light surrounding the Qallupiluq like a thing alive.

The calf! The Qallupiluq screamed within its mind, even as the chimera's mouth loosed a true scream; for the blue light, the flame that emanated from the child, was a *qaumaniq*, the aura wielded by the Some Seen. This child, then, was an *Angakkuq*.

A Shaman.

How had the Qallupiluq not seen it before?

The child's qaumaniq seemed to assail the Qallupiluq from all sides, as dogs will harry a bear; and the pain of the Angakkuq light bit like thousandfold teeth. The Qallupiluq fell, and merciful blackness engulfed the chimera for a time. When the Qallupiluq was again conscious of its surroundings, it found that its Human shape had dissolved, leaving the chimera in blissful formlessness. The water of the ice-crack was liquid once again, and the sea seemed to beckon. The child Angakkuq had departed.

The dog had returned, sitting, watching with eyes of palest yellow.

"Laugh at my weakness," the Qallupiluq said. "I know that's what you've come to do."

"No," the dog said, "I've come to deliver the message of my master, the child you would have taken. She is an Angakkuq, as you have learned to your agony. But you must also know that she is the daughter of the girl you took by the ice-crack years ago. She bears her mother's name, and therefore something of her mother's anirniq, that life-breath which you would have stolen."

"So this is revenge," the Qallupiluq said, and the chimera

chuckled without humour. "What now, Helper? Do you finish me here? Or am I to be the Angakkuq's next slave?"

"She would never have you as a Helper," the dog replied, "and your destruction would not satisfy her. I have come to place her command upon you, Qallupiluq: that you are to return to the sea, to throw yourself upon the mercy of *Nuliajuq*, she who is the greatest Agony of the deep. The Deep Mother, then, will be your judge."

The Qallupiluq's laughter was pained. "Then I am destroyed," the chimera said. "The Mother cannot forgive me. I have slain the whales for pleasure, the seals for sport. And they are her children."

The dog stood up, its eyes burning. "You," the Helper answered, "who use 'sin' as an excuse to commit evil, now claim to understand the workings of forgiveness? The Deep Mother was a girl once, and understands more of Human ways than you might guess. This is your punishment, Qallupiluq: to have what you have denied others."

"Forgiveness!" the Qallupiluq cried out, just as the power of the Angakkuq took hold of it, driving the chimera toward the deeps. "What Strength is there in such a little thing?"

But the dog was gone.

OIL

For now, Suqqivaa sighed, her needle dipping in and out of seal-skin. Her husband was Irnginnak, and he was once again flatter-ing his youngest wife, never sparing a glance for Suqqivaa herself. Suqqivaa was the man's oldest wife, and she knew that, as long as that younger wife was around, he would never touch her.

Suqqivaa glanced over at her *qulliq*, the soapstone lamp that served as her emblem of womanhood, providing light and warmth throughout the winter. It was now well into the moon time of *Aagjulirvik*, so that all lived under domes of snow, await-ing the return of sunlit days. Suqqivaa noticed that the tiny line of jacinth flames, burning evenly at the edge of the lamp, was growing low. She set aside her clothing repairs for a moment, searching for a skin container so as to add more seal oil to the lamp's stone pan. As she did so, she paused, once again admiring her little lamp: the lovely striations of olive ran through and over a richer green stone, so that the object seemed almost alive. She ran her finger over its viridescent bands, as though the lamp itself had begged for her touch. And she forgot, for a moment, about the oil.

"What are you doing?" her husband demanded. A moment ago, Irnginnak had been sitting next to his younger wife, tickling and forcing giggles out of the girl as she pretended to do her own work. She was shameless, it seemed, inviting Irnginnak's touch as easily as the lamp had invited Suqqivaa's own. The younger wife sat silent, now, staring ahead while Irnginnak took the moment to address his oldest bride.

"Up to something," Irnginnak rumbled. "Always up to something."

Suqqivaa made no answer, but simply ignored her husband, using a short stick to pick at the line of flames along her lamp's edge. Some had gone out, making it all the more urgent that she find that container of oil.

"So, you're ignoring me now," Irnginnak added, facing only his oldest wife's shoulder. "Did you think I didn't see you being lazy? You know I need that," he said, pointing at the clothing Suqqivaa had been repairing, "ready for when I next go out. But you like to stare into that lamp, don't you? You're ugly as a hag, but lazy as a child."

Suqqivaa merely smiled, for the harshness had ceased to sting her long ago. In those earlier days, when she'd been a new bride, Irnginnak's remarks had made her feel like less than a dog. He spoke to her, after all, in the same way he spoke to his dog team—those poor creatures that had given him the greatest practice at honing cruelty. He had owned many dogs back then, when his sled had first arrived at her parents' camp; when he'd arrogantly requested her as a bride. Young men, it seemed, needed wives. Some wives were purportedly taken for pleasure, or even for the sake of love (though that was a concept strange to Suqqivaa); but many brides were apparently claimed in order to supply young fools with slaves who could sew.

Suqqivaa had tried to refuse becoming a sewing slave.

Her parents had been proud *Angakkuit*: specialists in those forces dwelling beyond normal understanding. There had been a time when all camp dwellers had feared her mother and father; when the camp folk had approached one or both, heads lowered and humble, to ask their assistance against otherworldly entities. It had been Suqqivaa's ardent wish that she, too, could learn the skills of her parents, so that she might share in that respect. And her parents, delighted, had taught her—up till Irnginnak's arrival. Then it had all been talk about duty, tradition; as well as that ultimate fact of Suqqivaa's family status: her mother had borne her late in life. Suqqivaa's parents had been aged, and they'd no longer been able to afford support for a daughter.

Suqqivaa had sworn to them, then, that she would rather have lived alone than go with a husband. She had begged them to spare her the humiliation of marriage, asked if she might simply live apart and support herself, visiting occasionally, rather than going away with a man.

Yet her parents had silenced her, insisting that all was in order. This was the way in which things had to be done.

"I didn't know I was lazy," Suqqivaa told her husband. She tried to keep the anger out of her tone, but failed. "If you would rather grope your prettier wife, instead of hunting," she added, "why can't I at least fondle my lamp?"

Irnginnak, face reddening at her words, stood and started toward her. Suqqivaa flinched, feeling like a fool for her words, and she wondered, in a detached sort of way, if he would actually strike her. But her answer came when Irnginnak froze, standing over her with arm upraised toward a backhand blow, and she saw his widened eyes.

Irnginnak was staring at Suqqivaa's lamp, his expression one of newfound horror. Then he stepped back, breathing fast, gaze flicking back and forth between Suqqivaa and the lamp.

"You're evil," he told his oldest wife.

Suqqivaa said nothing, but only sighed.

"You're trying to will evil at me," Irnginnak maintained. "You think I don't remember your parents? How they were Angakkuit? You will nothing but evil on me."

Suqqivaa scowled, indicating *no* with her features. "I don't want any evil for you, my husband," she told him. "No good, either. I just don't care enough to think about you. Not at all."

"You suppose you're clever," Irnginnak said after a moment. Then he pointed at Suqqivaa's lamp. "But your qulliq betrays you. I see your evil there. Reflected in its stone."

Suqqivaa frowned, then stared at her lamp for a moment. "I see nothing," she said, turning back to her husband.

"Lies!" Irnginnak roared. "There's a face in it! Burning eyes! A tongue!"

Then the man squinted, leaning forward as though to second-guess whatever he'd witnessed of the lamp. Still, he would not approach it.

"It was there," he said in a quiet voice. Then Irnginnak returned to the side of his younger wife, whose girlish hands rose to stroke his heavy cheeks. "It was," Irnginnak murmured in a petulant way, still eyeing the lamp and Suqqivaa. "I'm not mad."

"Of course not, husband," Suqqivaa said, glad that his outrageous behaviour had subsided for the moment.

Suqqivaa began to seek for the oil again, glad that she had not experienced one more blow. Still, as she glanced up to espy the younger wife stroking her husband, she realized she'd have taken a thousand, rather than let Irnginnak touch her in any softer way. He had claimed his conjugal rights—as he and tradition apparently saw them—only once. It had been soon after the man had stolen Suqqivaa away from her parents. She had not yet ceased to weep out her new anguish, and the tears had stood fresh in her eyes, when groping hands had sought her in bed. She remembered rolling away, then rolling again, pulling her limbs inward as though to compress them into her very torso. She had never known that muscles could sit rigid for so long. Her best memory, however, was the smell of the man: the pungency of aged walrus, his favourite treat, with which he had stuffed himself before seeking her. She recalled vomiting at his touch; and of how the two admixed scents had seemed to follow her for days. To the present, she was unable to smell walrus without gagging.

Suqqivaa's heart began to race. Where was the oil? Without it, her lamp flames would weaken unto death. Under her breath, she chastised herself for leaving it so long unattended.

"Don't you think I don't see you," Irnginnak spoke to her back.

Suqqivaa clamped her teeth together, still searching amid piled caribou hides. How could she have been so careless?

"Always plotting," Irnginnak went on behind her. "Always scheming. Not like this pretty one here," he added, referring to his younger wife, who loosed a thin giggle. "She's my real wife, Suqqivaa. You know that? She's the real one."

Trying to think of Irnginnak's comments as one might regard summer mosquito whines, Suqqivaa rose to search about the *iglu*. It was a mess, crammed with half-completed tools, scraps of hide, and other bric-a-brac. Irnginnak liked it that way, despite all of Suqqivaa's attempts to order it.

"I need wives who support me," Irnginnak droned on, "not bring me down. Every hunter understands the idea of support, Suqqivaa. Do you?"

With little rooting about, Suqqivaa at last found the skin jug of oil. She rose and turned with it in hand, letting out a startled gasp when she was blocked by Irnginnak.

With dire stealth, the man had arisen from his seated position. He now stood between Suqqivaa and the lamp. He showed large, yellowed teeth, one of which had gone black, in a mock-grin. He was close enough to have bitten down, with them, upon her face.

"You know what we say when we don't like a hunter,

Suqqivaa?" he asked her. "We say 'I should take him seal hunting.' That's what we say."

Suqqivaa felt the gooseflesh arise on her skin at the murderous reference; but she met her husband's gaze. His eyes were not entirely focused, and seemed to look through her, as though he were instead regarding some medium in which she swam.

"Would you like that, old wife?" he asked her. "Would you like me to take you seal hunting?"

With great care, breath suspended in throat, Suqqivaa stepped around her husband. The man did not turn, nor did his dark eyes track her movement; but she nevertheless walked as if she were in the presence of a white bear.

In absolute quietude, she managed to get to her lamp, where, with one fluid motion and not sparing a second, she poured more oil, thick, translucent, into the stone pan. She did not bother to replace the bottle, nor even to worry about some oil dripping from the mouth and over her fingers, but held it while using a stick in the opposite hand to coax up the waning flames. Feeling as though she might feel a blow to her skull at any moment, perhaps a muscular arm about her neck, she made her vision—her very mind—one with the little orange lights. Soon, they formed a perfect row, neither starved nor glutted with oil.

In the corner of one eye, Suqqivaa saw her husband return to where he'd been sitting. Then, she heard the cooing, the uxorious praise, the kisses showered upon the younger wife. And the relieved breath seemed to shiver in her throat.

In staring at her qulliq, Suqqivaa saw its striations stretch and warp, until a vague face manifested in the side of the lamp. This was, she knew, her helper entity—that mind which resided in the qulliq. The helper's eyes, glaring from the stone of the lamp, burned like embers. Its glowing tongue licked forth from open mouth, while the row of saffron flames stood like prickling hairs over its brow. It always behaved in this way, showing itself and alternately grinning or scowling, when it wanted to thank her for

oil. It used the same mixture of expressions to remind her that it was starved.

As the face receded once again into stone, Suqqivaa brushed a finger across its cheek. She needed no longer fear Irnginnak's ire, nor even his attention. For when the lamp was well fuelled, his mind was fully enslaved to the false younger wife that Suqqivaa had long ago asked her helper to create. It had always been Suqqivaa's hope that, with Irnginnak's wits focused on a more desirable bride, she could in time store up enough supplies to make fleeing feasible. As long as she kept herself from such close calls as this one, and kept the lamp's powers well fed with oil, there might yet come a day when Irnginnak returned from hunting—and found all his wives, real or false, gone.

For now, Suqqivaa sighed, her needle dipping in and out of sealskin. Her husband was Irnginnak, and he was once again flattering his youngest wife, never sparing a glance for Suqqivaa herself. Suqqivaa was the man's oldest wife, and she knew that, as long as that younger wife was around, he would never touch her.

THE FINAL CRAFT

Suvirpaa stood in his sanctum, magenta eyes flicking back and forth between looming panels of diamond. The panels showed events as they unfolded across the wide Land: in snow-mottled hills, the whorls of glaciers, jagged ice-pans of the sea—even far below these things, in the place where Suvirpaa's people were dying.

A Human might have termed Suvirpaa's sanctum a cavern, though it had been carven with nothing other than deliberation, in homage to the deep earthen forms, the striations of rock and warp of mineral formation, that Suvirpaa's folk so admired. A Human, reaching for other understandable analogues, might also have called Suvirpaa a man. He was not, for his kind knew nothing of male or female, any more than they understood the softness of flesh or the surge of blood in artery. Suvirpaa's body, as with the rest of his folk, instead consisted of multitudinous fibres, so minute and densely packed that their individuality defied the naked eye, appearing on the surface like a strange kind of stone which moved as of heavy leather. And, while Suvirpaa's people might have resembled the cold stone that was their age-old womb and home, their fibres seethed with the stuff of alternate life, bearing a heat beyond any Human hearth.

If a Human had accused Suvirpaa's heart of now breaking, however, he might have agreed.

Suvirpaa glanced, once more, at a diamond panel in which laboured a true man: one of the Human males, the squat and fleshly folk who had dwelt so long on the surface. The man's clothes, constructed from a caribou's hide, displayed ragged fringes that flapped in the chill surface wind. Suvirpaa watched as the man hefted a stone, perhaps half the size of his own torso, teeth parting in an unheard gasp of effort. As though trying not to cause damage to that which he constructed, the man struggled, placing the stone on top of two others with an obvious measure of reverence. These greater stones were already balanced atop two shorter rock-piles, so that the whole had come to resemble the lower part of a standing body. The builder straightened for a moment, wiping at his brow with the back of a sleeve, then stooped to adjust the growing cairn.

"A man of the Human Ones," a voice came from behind Suvirpaa. Suvirpaa did not turn, recognizing it as that of his colleague, Kinguvaanguqatigiik. "They still believe," Kinguvaanguqatigiik added. "They believe we will bring them assistance."

Only at these last few words did Suvirpaa turn, but Kinguvaanguqatigiik's roseate gaze would not meet Suvirpaa's own, instead holding fast to those images conveyed by the panel above. Except for the eyes, Suvirpaa's colleague was identical to himself. The visitor stood holding twin tablets, slabs of banded onyx whose subtle shades ever danced.

"The men and women have always had faith," Suvirpaa maintained, before turning back to the panel's imagery.

Kinguvaanguqatigiik made no immediate reply, but instead stood with Suvirpaa for a time, watching the labours of the Human. The man had, by now, found slimmer, longer rocks that resembled outstretched arms, and these he placed with care atop the structure he'd already created. Then he reached down to find "shoulders"—comprised of a single flat stone he had earlier put aside for the purpose.

"I find your phrasing inappropriate," Kinguvaanguqatigiik at last said.

Suvirpaa but half-turned, issuing a guttural chuckle. "Do you?" he asked. He was little surprised by his colleague's observation. Suvirpaa's statement, after all, had been born of sentiment; and his folk, after all, were distrustful of obvious emotion. Passion was acceptable as part of the natural order. But allowing it to find voice was considered vulgar. Suvirpaa was only surprised by the fact that Kinguvaanguqatigiik had bothered with such protocol. Here and now, so close to the end?

"Yes," Suvirpaa's colleague said after a moment. "I find your references to faith inappropriately religious."

This was an insult: millennia ago, Suvirpaa's people had purged themselves of religious delusion. Traditionally, religiosity was deemed symptomatic of inferior mentality.

Suvirpaa sighed. "Everything about our folk has been religious, hasn't it?" he asked Kinguvaanguqatigiik. At once, Suvirpaa gestured toward the scene in the diamond panel. "Is it not proven, by way of us playing at divinity for so long?" he pressed his colleague. "Have we not used our artifice to imitate the voice of spirit? Authored instrumentation to work sign and wonder among the Human Ones? Altered culture with prophecy and anagoge?"

"Toward pragmatic ends," Kinguvaanguqatigiik insisted. "For the sake of the Land. The natural order."

"Natural order?" Suvirpaa asked, mocking his peer with another dry chuckle. "Natural order now arrives at our very beds, Kinguvaanguqatigiik." Suvirpaa gestured toward the only portal to his sanctum, a high door of ruby inlaid with rainbow ammolite histories. "Step outside," Suvirpaa went on, "and it will claim you

in short time. I can show you your 'natural order' even now."

"Suvirpaa, don't!" hissed Kinguvaanguqatigiik.

Yet Suvirpaa had already projected his will into the instrumentation around him. His beloved tools knew him, knew his thoughts well, for they were the means by which his will was translated into architecture. By now, they had allowed him to shape innumerable grand vaults and winding passages—all the places in which Suvirpaa's folk had once thrived. All now lifeless. As ever, the instrumentation responded to the familiarity of Suvirpaa's mind, its thousandfold jewels and coloured facets shifting like a living, nitid mass.

One of the diamond panels offered a perspective that flew in mad circles over the muddied landscape of a glacier. The perspective shifted under Suvirpaa's will. It darkened, displaying a gloomy chamber, long and empty tables lit only by turning lights of various colours, weary hues cast from somewhere near the unseen ceiling.

As Suvirpaa and his peer stared, wordless, the passing seconds revealed shadows. Alive, they seemed to slink and undulate in the darker places between and underneath the tables. Occasionally, one reared to reveal itself as a series of ebon bladders, limbs like lightless, writhing gouts. The faces of the creatures, foetal and mouthless, featured great luminous eyes, round and devoid of intellect. These silvern orbs framed the one feature with which the horrors sought back and forth, up and down in all directions: a kind of horn, long and lean, like a twisted spout of oil.

A long moment passed, in which neither Suvirpaa or his colleague could find words. No animate being in the history of their folk had managed to educe such terror in their breasts, and Suvirpaa immediately regretted his own emotional reaction: the frustration over Kinguvaanguqatigiik's words, which had impelled him to call up this view. He did not want to see these things. Not so deep in his home. Not like this. Not even to prove a point.

"Turn it off," Kinguvaanguqatigiik muttered.

Suvirpaa moved his will to do so, but not before he was interrupted by an alteration in the scene. As he and his peer watched, their bodies vibrating with horror like two struck crystals, another one of their folk ran into the chamber. Each of Suvirpaa's folk knew every other—so he and Kinguvaanguqatigiik recognized the runner. Out of respect for the fact that he was doomed, however, neither uttered his name.

The runner paused part of the way into the chamber, noticing the shadows that of a sudden seethed toward him. He glanced back the way he'd come, only to find his pursuers—more of the creatures—issuing like streams of black vomit from the passageway.

Understanding his situation, the runner backed himself against a wall. There he sat, legs crossed, head lowered, resigned and waiting.

From every direction of the chamber, tides of the things flowed in, horns at tilt and bob in the varihued light of the ceiling. Further, Suvirpaa could see changes in the wall above the victim: cracks in the stone widening, puddings of ebon spilling forth, luminous eyes opening to fix upon the sup that had drawn them.

Suvirpaa, regaining his concentration, willed the panel back to its previous glacier view. Like all his few remaining folk, he knew how it ended: black limbs encircling, squeezing; luminous eyes fluttering in admixed lust and ecstasy; drilling horns seeking, aligning themselves, at last piercing the head for deep drink.

"I didn't know the *Ikuutarjuit* were so . . . numerous," Suvirpaa whispered. He wept, as he spoke, in the tearless way of his kind, with deep, inward shudders that lay beyond the naked eye.

"The Drillers Ravin have penetrated into every chamber," Kinguvaanguqatigiik said, "that open stone affords. They squeeze through, widen by their way, even the most minute of fissures."

"Is that why you're here?" Suvirpaa asked after a moment. "You've been sent to see if the Final Craft is finished?"

Though Suvirpaa had always deemed the name "Final Craft" foolish, it described the master project the rest of his kind felt would save their remaining numbers from the Drillers. When the Ikuutarjuit had first ascended from the deep stone where not even Suvirpaa's kind would venture, the Drillers had been little more than some lurid enigma—of which the Land produced many. But then had come the days of their spread: their invasion of vaults in which Suvirpaa's kind had walked, unmolested, since time immemorial. They had spread even to the surface, to the waters and the open Land, unfazed by either winter winds or summer sun. Early attempts to kill the Drillers, using some forms of instrumentation that Suvirpaa himself had devised, were successful, however costly. Their nature had ever defied the best of inquiry, and their numbers had ever swollen. At last had arrived the darkest days, when the sentinels of Suvirpaa's people had withered and fallen back, then back again, and the Drillers Ravin had followed.

It was by the time Suvirpaa's folk were approximately halved in number, that the remainder drew him into council. He had always been the most innovative of his kind, and he was urged to develop a series of cysts in the deep rock, layered about with materials of his own choosing, to serve as a shelter for his remaining folk. This, then, would be the Final Craft—a place without opening or thinnest fissure, where the last of Suvirpaa's people might escape extinction under the Drillers.

"Have you finished the Final Craft?" Kinguvaanguqatigiik pressed.

Suvirpaa did not at first answer. He simply stared at the panel in which the Human One, having found a round stone nearly as large as his own skull, was finishing his creation. He positioned the rock over the "shoulders" of the man-like cairn, so that it topped the work off in serving as a "head." In witnessing the creation, Suvirpaa smiled deep in his breast, and something in him seemed to run with rich heat. The stone was beautiful, by any standard, chosen for its bright green striations, banding it round between fields of blue-black ticking. It seemed to shine even on the muted Land beneath cloud cover.

The Human One stepped back, turning his head this way and that. Then he hopped someway down the hill, on which the creation was situated. He stepped all about, circling the hill, checking his stone-man from every angle. Then he stepped up to stand next to it, once again, placing a beaten and weathered hand on it as on the shoulder of a companion. He smiled, just a bit, before sitting in rest. Somehow, Suvirpaa felt as though he himself were resting with him.

"I find it extremely crass of you to watch one of our servants while I pose such a vital question," Kinguvaanguqatigiik commented.

"Our servants?" Suvirpaa asked, now turning from the display in true anger. "They have served us, Kinguvaanguqatigiik. But they're not our servants. You yourself spout on about natural order. But would we have managed this order, regulated its temperance and negotiated its imbalances, without their assistance? They have never known us. But they've ever honoured us—*loved* us—because they trust that ours is the voice of the Land itself. This *inukshuk*," Suvirpaa added, indicating the structure the Human One had built, "is one small facet of the rituals we've taught them. We have secreted messages into the minds of their wisest. Whispered, via instrumentation, into their dreams. So that their wisdom becomes an expression of our knowledge. Thus have we guarded the Land alongside them for untold years. Encouraged its life. Prevented destructive change. And, though they've never seen my face or yours, they have never questioned our lead. How can you call them mere 'servants' when they display such faith? We are criminal, while they are lawful. We are disloyal, while they are true. And, cowards, we would bury ourselves in some Final Craft while the Drillers make food of them."

Kinguvaanguqatigiik, who had begun to rock in irritation from the mention of "love," drew his onyx tablets closer to himself. "It is disloyal to your own kind," he said, "to use such words in describing us. We have given all we may to the men and women. They, along with the Land, have profited by our subtle guidance. The Drillers Ravin are now upon us all. If the Human Ones, as you say, gain some strength via their faith, let this rarefied concept see them through. As for us, we must resort to our own methodology. Therefore, I repeat, have you developed the Final Craft?"

Suvirpaa stood quivering for some time, never having experienced such candescent rage, such disgust over the empty hearts of those he called his own. After minutes had elapsed, he became aware of what had so muted him. It was not the anger. It was shame. Simple and rancid shame.

Yet, in time, in staring at his waiting peer, Suvirpaa managed an answer:

"I have."

"Then I shall leave you to your pet," Kinguvaanguqatigiik said, pointing to the image of the Human One, "and soon expect a report on how, on *when*, we are to sequester ourselves in your new shelter. Be glad, master artificer," Kinguvaanguqatigiik added after a moment's pause. "Perhaps the surface folk will go extinct, as other animals have in ages past. Such things are regrettable, but not all tragedies may be averted. At least we, the grander folk, will continue on. Perhaps there will even be folk such as the Human Ones still existent when we next emerge. If you seem overly attached to them, then let it be recorded that such emotionality simply reflects the stress of your heroic efforts."

Suvirpaa made no answer, and watched his colleague depart via the ruby-ammolite door.

For several minutes, Suvirpaa calmed himself, watching the Human One on his hill. The man was now moving his mouth, perhaps in a song, that strange expression of deep passion in which the men and women were sometimes known to engage.

Inwardly, Suvirpaa smiled, amazed at how the man seemed to sing at no more than the horizon. Had it been summer, an icy coast might have been in view from this hill. As it was, the man sang to a seemingly limitless expanse, a sheet like ivory admixed with whitest quartz—a view that allowed the mind to envision forever.

Of a sudden, the bitterness returned in all its strength, souring the well of Suvirpaa's being. The man's inukshuk, he knew, was a call: at once work of art and summons born of faith, going out to powers who would never again answer.

Then, seeking some hard edge within his core, Suvirpaa brushed his will across the instrumentation. All of the diamond panels above him, six in total, blushed magenta, before presenting various scenes from Suvirpaa's home. He wanted a last look at his favourite halls and arcades, those whose beauty made him most proud; though his present viewings were marred by the sight of bloated shadows, silvern eyes, and ebon drills seeking each crack and corner.

The panels went black.

Suvirpaa poured his will into the instrumentation, deporting his mind with those flavours of concept and icon that presaged any great symphony of artifice. As his mind had ever done in expectation of creating, it went into an ideal place, where those elements needed for the task arranged themselves like explosions in reverse, and all felt quite certain, even while somehow a bit sad.

Then Suvirpaa, greatest artificer of his kind, strained artifice and instrumentation, and wrought the Final Craft. Yet it was not the Final Craft the last of his people had envisioned. It was, instead, the only crafting that Suvirpaa could find fitting for his folk as they were now.

In Suvirpaa's home, even those places far from his vision, there arrived a great shudder. The shudder shook every floor, every ceiling and wall—and its vibration did not stop, but only grew to an admixed groan and wail, as if each mineral particle had given voice in answer to Suvirpaa's call. And then there was movement, a mad and gelatinous wavering of the collective stone, before it poured like melted tallow.

Here was Suvirpaa's final artifice, and the way in which he chose to answer his remaining folk: the deep places of the world swelled inward, stone becoming heatless liquid for a brief time, before it once again solidified. The grand vaults and winding passages, born of Suvirpaa's genius and pride, were unmade. When the living stone poured inward, it held all in its embrace—filling every hall and chamber, every passageway and pore. As well, it caught and held the Ikuutarjuit. Those dread Drillers Ravin that had occupied Suvirpaa's home were at last stayed. Trapped in lightless stone, they would remain forever immured—alongside of those last few of Suvirpaa's folk.

When Suvirpaa felt the stone swelling in around himself, at last breaking his mind's link with the instrumentation, his final thoughts were of the Human One on the hill. Suvirpaa was worried for him. There were still those Drillers remaining on the surface, and Suvirpaa had no idea if the men and women could survive even a few. Yet Suvirpaa had done his best to author some last transmissions to that Human Folk. With his will like a great wind, Suvirpaa had sent out the most precious embers of ideation possessed by his own people, imaginings that would find their way into nothing other than dream. These sendings, their source unknown and arising as simple creativity in whatever minds might house them, would assist the Human Ones in enduring the Land. In understanding it. In guarding it, if they so chose.

Dreams might have constituted feeble gifts, yet they were all Suvirpaa could manage. His own folk had lived too long, their hearts growing colder than the Land's darkest bowels. It was time, perhaps, for surface men and women to bear the imaginings of those who had once played at divinity.

Suvirpaa tried not to feel embarrassed, before darkness descended, at the idea that his last artifice had been wrought of faith.

THE MOON LORD'S CALL

Many are the Animal Folk, most of whom have lasted out the Land's darker times by holding to their own laws. There are none among them more fond of law than the *Igutaapiit*, those of the Bee Folk. Proud and martial of bearing, the Igutaapiit are at once the most private of the animal peoples. So it was a marked time in the Land's long-ago when the Elders of the Hidden *Sanavik*—that living centre of Animal Folk law—asked the Bee Folk to represent them on the Moon; and the Igutaapiit agreed.

Now, it would take a great deal of time to travel straight from the surface of the Land to that of the Moon, and the journey—airless, chill, and black—would ravage the flesh of any creature who dared such a route. Yet there is a Strength, often invisible, that runs through all things; and the wisest of the Animal Folk had found, of old, one or two of those many secret paths connecting the Moon's Strength to that of the Land. It was by one of these ways, like some vast and invisible artery between spheres, that a party of four Igutaapiit travelled. They appeared on the moon almost instantly, as one might move from one chamber to the next, and the four came to stand under a great starry dome.

The Igutaapiit sisters were alarmed at what they saw before them, and they brandished weapons: some akin to spears of twisted lightning, others like thinnest blades, rippling like sun upon water. All warriors of the Igutaapiit sisterhood were well versed in their use. Yet their weapons now seemed feeble, inadequate to the vast creature looming from the centre of the chamber: here was a colossal dog, owning wild eyes and rust-hued fur, and it sat at the heart of a translucent spire of ice, towering twice as high as the dog it seemed to imprison. The dog, when it noticed the tiny Bee Folk before it, leaped to its feet, setting up a fevered howling. It scratched at its icy prison from within, yet its howls were muted by the ice around it.

"That is Singuuri," one of the Igutaapiit told her sisters. Her name was Pikkaq, and she was counted as the wisest of those making up the Bee Folk delegation. But for the blue-silver cord, a sort of headband across her almost perfectly bee-like head, she was identical to her sisters—standing upright upon chitinous legs, her torso brindled with fur both black and saffron, and holding her preferred weapon in the stronger pair of her fourfold arms. She seemed to clutch at her weapon, a living snarl of lightning, as though in agitation, adding:

"I remember the songs about Singuuri. The Moon Dog. We should move on. Before we hear his howls."

The party began to traverse the chamber, their light steps kicking up little puffs of dust as they went. As Pikkaq and the others made a wide circle around the still-frenzied (but thankfully imprisoned) dog, one of the sisters stopped to stare.

"But why is he imprisoned in . . . is it ice?" the one sister asked. Her name was Tuki, and she was counted as the least wise of those making up the Bee Folk delegation. She carried two short blades, like pieces cut from water awash with sun. Using one of these instruments, she tapped at the foot of the dog's iceberg-prison.

Some of the sisters half-turned, calling back to Tuki, using the concerted drone with which the Bee Folk traditionally admonish one another.

"But—" Tuki started.

"Follow," Pikkaq commanded. "Singuuri's howls will soon melt the ice. If we're here when the dog emerges, those same sounds will drive us mad." Pikkaq's voice betrayed some irritation, for the Igutaapiit find excessive speech wasteful, and curiosity the height of foolishness.

Tuki looked again, now noticing an outward-spreading pool of moisture about the ice-prison's base, and she jumped back before its edge touched her insectile feet. Water, she noticed, ran freely down the structure's surface, and the dog had nearly scratched its way through the thin remainder. Still, like most of her folk, it took much to make her fearful. Instead, she clashed her small and decorative wings together in agitation.

The Igutaapiit party had continued on without Tuki, hurrying in response to Pikkaq's urging. Tuki took a moment to catch up with her leader, and she immediately began to badger her.

"But this is not where we were supposed to go," Tuki said to Pikkaq. "You don't find this all wrong?"

"No," Pikkaq said with an indulgent sigh, "Singuuri's here to frighten away unwanted guests. Our folk, however, are invited. You'll see far more bizarre things ahead of us, sister. Including one more challenge to our arrival, I think. Now shut up."

Pikkaq, it seemed, had spotted an exit from the chamber, and she led her sisters toward it. It was a towering doorway, covered over with an eerie sort of veil, like some black curtain stirred by phantom winds; and over its vastness swirled crimson clouds, like blood in water. Tuki wondered, as she approached its great height, if it was really an opening, for it was easy to imagine that it led only to the embrace of darkness and void. Anxious, she ground her blades against each other, until a couple of her sisters droned for her to stop.

The great veil turned out to be illusory, as Pikkaq strode straight through its bottom. Unflinching, her Igutaapiit sisters followed, so that they all stood in a passageway apparently wrought—like the dome under which Singuuri was held—of starry night sky. Another towering veil, twin to the first, lay some distance ahead.

"Ridiculous," Pikkaq muttered in some frustration. "We're guests. Yet there's no allowance for our preferred size. Unless we want to remain underfoot in a place of giants, we must adapt. We need to be larger."

Without words, the sisters agreed and collectively bent their heads. They were not pleased with having to change, for of all the Animal Folk, the Igutaapiit most prefer to lean toward the physicality of the animal, rather than that alternate form of the Human One. Yet all can, when the demand is upon them, access something of the *innua*: the Human-like stuff they normally wear on their insides; and can force this substance to the outer skin. Such change is a holy thing, a sacred thing, to all of the Animal Folk, and therefore private. So the sisters looked away from each other as they focused, and sang sharp little songs to themselves. When the change at last came, their bodies ran first like melting fat, then oil on water, then at last like sunlight regarded past tears. And there seemed to come a shudder, then a sigh, from the collective Strength between them. And when they again regarded one another, they were changed.

The greatest change that had come over the sisters was that of size. All stood at more than half the height of the once-vaulting veils—perhaps about as tall as an adolescent child among the Human Folk. Also, their bee-eyes, once like twin, jewel-encrusted bowls upon their heads, had seemed to diminish and move farther apart; in each, a vague whiteness, hinting at a Human eye, seemed to glow from the centre. The bristles over the bodies of all were now true hair, luxuriant with black and saffron patterns; and the digits gripping weapons were fivefold, thumb and four fingers covered over with tight ebon skin.

Still wordless, the sisters strode through the next veil, and into the chamber beyond.

This chamber, too, was a dome, though it was not wrought of night sky, as the dome of Singuuri had been. Its ceiling was instead a black expanse, across which thousandfold hues seemed to flit and mock at play like living things. The dome was much larger than the one that had preceded it, though the sisters were little impressed. Their size was far greater than it had been before, and they were further distracted by the chamber's occupants.

Semi-circular benches ran round the circumference of the chamber. On these sat various beings, perhaps three dozen in total. Many, had they been standing, might have measured at half again the current size of the Igutaapiit, for the height of the Human Folk seemed the standard in this place. None, however, seemed to notice the entrance of the Bee Folk party, and all sat either rocking or stiller than stone, nursing gruesome, bloodless wounds: missing eyes, missing arms, missing legs, even missing viscera.

Many, Tuki realized as she brandished her blades, should have been dead.

"Put your weapons away," Pikkaq commanded. "If I remember, this is the place of Aagjuk. We must remain for her song. Endure it. But don't listen to the words. Sit."

Pikkaq started to walk over to a bench, presumably to sit, and two of the sisters followed. Tuki tried to stop her leader, then, to ask various questions about the place, but Pikkaq merely brushed her sister aside. Furious and sullen, Tuki stamped over to one of the few open spaces on a bench, and she sat facing the centre of the chamber.

Barely had Tuki seated herself, when a voice to her right whispered:

"Aagjuk will dance now, and sing. But for Creation's sake, block your ears!"

Tuki straightened in her seat when she noticed that the creature next to her was a man of the Human Folk. As with many in this chamber, he should have been dead. Since he was shirtless, Tuki could see the great hollow where his abdomen had been cut away. His intestines, along with his feet, had gone missing.

"I listened," the man went on. "I don't know how long ago. But I listened, and laughed. And then she took my guts. Now I can't stop listening. Thousand upon thousand songs and I can't stop."

Before Tuki could ask anything of the man, who was now weeping, another voice hissed to her left, "He's a fool. A weakling. Aagjuk's song is beauty. If we are lucky, this time, she'll prophesy for us."

The speaker was a woman, another one of the Human Folk, though she possessed neither hands nor eyes. She giggled as she spoke.

"She's gone mad," the first speaker, the man, told Tuki. "Take my advice, or you'll end up like her."

"Coward!" the blind woman said with a snicker. "Aagjuk's lesson lies in the flesh! She takes these small things, and leaves us with wisdom!"

Tuki clacked her blades together (she had refused the order to put them away), saying, "The only thing this Aagjuk will take from me is pain. She will draw back her own stump if she makes to touch one of the Igutaapiit."

"Blasphemy!" the blind, handless woman gasped.

"You're the craziest one here," the gutless man hissed at Tuki, "if you think you can fight Aagjuk. She's a lesser A'aa, but still in that grand company of Agonies. Put your weapons aside! You'll have to endure something of her song before you can *think* of leaving."

Upon the man's words, Tuki felt a damp emotion, almost akin to fear, touch upon her heart. As one of the Bee Folk, such passions were remote and dim to her, the equivalent of stark terror in most other beings. Only an A'aa, or some similar entity, could come so close to educing dread in Tuki's kind. There was no Strength of the Animal Folk, not even among the most powerful Elders, that approached what ran in the veins of the Agonies. They were the great movers, of old, whose imaginings and tantrums shifted Creation. Even the surroundings about Tuki now, she knew, were real only because that master mind which ruled the Moon had willed them to be. If it were true that Aagjuk was an A'aa, even a pale shadow of the greater Agonies, there would be no defying her.

There was no further discussion, for the victims to either side of Tuki fell silent as Aagjuk entered the dome.

To Tuki, the sight of the vaunted Aagjuk was disappointing. The purportedly awesome being wore the form of an aged, fat woman of the Human Folk. Her clothes, too, were as those of the Human Folk, though not nearly as well made: mere tatters of soiled caribou hide. The tatters waved to the same rhythm as the patchy strands of her long grey hair; and she dragged a great dun bag in the dust, waddling her way to the centre of the room. There, she brushed some of her hair aside, revealing a heavy, wrinkled face, her massive grin beaming moonlike under round cheeks and burning eyes. It seemed, at first, that she wore a strange kind of makeup over her entire face; or tattoos; though Tuki realized after a moment that the colours upon Aagjuk's skin were on the move. Perhaps, Tuki thought, the hues were *part* of the crone's skin; they seemed innumerable and ever-shifting, and Tuki quickly realized that they were alike to those colours at play across the ceiling above.

The crone turned to that half of the chamber where the Igutaapiit had seated themselves, and her already impressive grin spread to grotesque wideness. Always, Aagjuk held the edge of her bag in one hand, while the other hand remained concealed within it.

"Beautiful!" Aagjuk cried in a shuddering voice, taking a step toward the Igutaapiit. "Beautiful! Beautiful! To have such beautiful guests! And I have such beautiful presents for you all! I could never be so rude, though, as to sling presents around, without singing in welcome first! No, I would never be so rude! You must listen, then, to my beautiful little song! Then you will have your presents!"

As Tuki watched, bracing herself for the ordeal, Aagjuk raised one foot, then the other. These actions, Aagjuk repeated, raising right, left, right, left, and so on, with a timing that was perfect and somehow fascinating to watch. In this way she began to rock, all the while emitting a low croon, and still smiling at her "guests." After a few moments of this dance, she began to move about the chamber, turning and rocking in her strange, moaning performance; and as Aagjuk turned back to the silent Bee Folk, words at last came:

Lend me some taste of steady self,
That you may know an echo wise.
For mad is never chill as fear,
Nor fear hollow as heedless mind.

Tuki was barely aware of Aagjuk's words, for she had brought her own reserves of Strength to surround her awareness like a cocoon, dimming her consciousness—if not her ears—to the crone's strange song. Even so, Tuki's Strength was barely sufficient to the task, and she kept her eyes averted, fixed upon the dust of the floor. While she did so, she sought ways to bolster that shield of Strength, distracting herself with every song she could remember of the Bee Folk traditions. There was no lack of such songs, and these Tuki sang under her breath, hoping that Aagjuk would soon end this bizarre test of wills. Time, however, seemed to slow itself as it flowed over and around the crone's words, as though it were Aagjuk's own ally.

And Tuki began to weaken.

At one point, Tuki's mind seemed to lose hold of the Bee Folk songs, though she knew that they numbered in the hundreds. She reined in her thoughts as best she could, using the techniques of discipline that the Igutaapiit had developed over millennia, yet all such artifice of a sudden withered in her mind. It was strange, but as the low drone of Aagjuk's voice seeped into the corners of her selfhood, Tuki found herself wanting to laugh. She could feel the mirth rising like some spinning, tickling ball from her very core. She wanted to let it loose, watching Aagjuk's rhythmic dance; laughing aloud at the crone's antics; and heeding the words of Aagjuk's song.

Listen, a smooth voice seemed to sough across her insides. *Listen. There will never come a song so important as this . . .*

Then Tuki looked up and there was Aagjuk, the colours of the crone's grinning face whirling, spangling, bleeding before her. Aagjuk stood within arm's length, rocking, singing, one hand yet hidden inside her vast bag; and Tuki knew, of a sudden, that no crone stood before her. Here, she sensed, danced only the image of an old woman—a mask that might as easily have resembled a mountain, or a tide, or glacier. Aagjuk was no being, but a force, deathless, bitter, and amused. Aagjuk's eyes, shining like two mad stars, were fixed upon Tuki's own, and Tuki no longer wished to resist hearing those words:

Who will have the ones unwanted?
The voids that know but lonely spark.
As well to guttle down the world,
And make of dream unending drink . . .

Aagjuk's words, when she seemed to understand that Tuki was at last listening, trailed off.

Eyes still upon Tuki's own, and Tuki yet hearing the words of the crone's song echoing across her mind, Aagjuk slowly withdrew her hand from where it had remained concealed in the bag. Tuki watched the motion, feeling somehow distanced from the sight, as though Aagjuk's actions were now but the events in a story.

"Beautiful gift," Aagjuk said in the softest voice, "for the beauty who listens . . . "

The crone withdrew, along with her hand, a long and narrow blade, black with aged blood.

Then Pikkaq was there, falling upon Aagjuk and knocking the crone aside. Aagjuk cried out with a feral sort of snarl, though her grin remained, and the two fell together into the dust, rolling, until Pikkaq seemed to gain the momentary advantage. The Bee warrior drove a knee into Aagjuk's roundness, though the crone hardly seemed to sense the blow. At once, Pikkaq seized the crone's wrist, holding her knife hand at bay. Before the Bee warrior could plunge her lance of lightning into Aagjuk's heart, however, the crone's eyes rolled within sickly orange flames. Something semi-visible, writhing like a ball of translucent worms, seemed to strike Pikkaq, hurling her off of Aagjuk.

As Tuki watched her leader ascend nearly to the ceiling, then drop in the dust, her mind was freed from Aagjuk's grip. Tuki seized her paired blades (not having realized, throughout Aagjuk's song, that she'd dropped them), and leapt to her feet. Her other sisters, too, were off the bench, stalking Aagjuk in a wide half-circle about the still-grinning crone.

"Flee!" Pikkaq cried, as she again rushed Aagjuk. She seemed to deliberately grapple with the crone, as though to keep her body between Aagjuk and her sisters.

"Go on to the next chamber!" Pikkaq urged again, though all the Igutaapiit sisters stood paralyzed with uncertainty. "We must not fail here!"

Tuki watched her sisters turn away from their leader, who yet struggled with the amused Aagjuk. After one further moment of indecision, Tuki also turned to seek the doorway leading to the next chamber. Her heart seemed to hang like torn strips within her—with guilt at allowing Pikkaq to sacrifice herself; with guilt at having made it necessary for Pikkaq to sacrifice herself. She had never wept, nor did she now, yet she had never known such sorrow.

As Tuki fled with her remaining sisters through the next veil, she flinched at the sound of Aagjuk's words behind her:

"Enough fun for now, beautiful one. You can have all the presents I wanted to give."

Pikkaq screamed.

Blessedly, the sound of Pikkaq's suffering was cut short as Tuki dashed through the veil, joining her sisters in the great hall beyond. In size, it dwarfed the domes through which the Igutaapiit had thus far passed, and the Bee sisters stood stunned—for here was the grand Court of Taqqiq, the Moon's true master.

Tuki knew: Taqqiq was one of those eldritch Agonies. As such, his whims and moods, his secret dreams, had wrought all she now beheld of the hall. She, along with Taqqiq's other guests, stood like a congregation of lice beneath tremendous vaulting and interconnecting domes of pearl. A maze of arches and oddly curved pillars, like the tusks of fallen giants, seemed to stretch off for as far as the eye could see. Peculiar lines, serrated, diagonal, seemed to zigzag high and low—and it took Tuki a long moment to realize that these were stairs, many appearing to cross paths, leading to places unseen. Everywhere, whether underfoot or across the soaring heights, flashed patterned inlays of platinum and rainbow ammolite; and these tended to lead the eye to grotesque sculptures, many nebulous and unfinished, that loomed like phantoms stretching forth from ceiling, wall, and pearlescent floor.

The Court of Taqqiq crawled with life as grotesque as the decor. The saner sorts of beings, Tuki noted, were those who walked in shapes akin to the Human Folk; though many of these figures were nevertheless distorted, having skin that moved as though unknown things wrestled beneath it; or eyes that alternately withered and renewed themselves in their sockets; or limbs that lengthened, then retracted, snaking in an eerily boneless way.

More disturbing were those beings far removed from either Animal or Human Folk. Tuki, along with her sisters, stepped aside to allow the passage of eleven creatures, each about Tuki's current size, resembling tattooed worms upon crane-like legs. The mouths of the things, faceless and kissing at the air with raw, red lips, swept left and right as the eleven went by. The spurs along their attenuated legs dripped burning blood with every step, hissing, steaming where droplets met the pearly floor. Tuki was entranced by the sight of the creatures, and they caused her to accidentally jostle a statuesque being in a trailing coat of murrey (or was it skin?). The lofty being, whose head resembled a spiralled horn more than anything that might hold a brain, issued a low trumpeting noise at Tuki; at once, it readjusted its leathery grip on a large, transparent globe (inside of this stood a miniature, cream-coloured bear, having seven spider's eyes). Tuki reeled away from the tall being, some guest who was obviously of poor temperament, and she was nearly tripped by something jellied and jewelled that flowed around her legs like frigid river water.

Tuki's two sisters then grabbed her by the arms and hauled her close to themselves, droning in displeasure. Once they had pulled her over to an open patch of floor, where they might stand for a moment without being trampled by grotesqueries, one of the sisters pointed over the heads of the crowd. Tuki could see, where her sister indicated, a distant area dominated by statues like majestic antlers of marble. There, the guests stood thick, and above them seemed to rear a twisting flame—silver, much like the Moon's own light.

"We're late," one of the sisters muttered.

"We've failed," the other sister added.

Tuki, who had been brought along for her skill at arms rather than her wisdom, had not been made privy to the Igutaapiit reason for appearing at Taqqiq's Court. She was therefore confused at the words of her sisters. Mostly, she was angered by them. She did not know why Pikkaq had sacrificed herself, ensuring that they'd made it to this place. But, in the wake of Pikkaq's sacrifice, the strange defeatism of the others seemed to degrade Pikkaq's very being.

"Why do you speak like traitors?" Tuki said, pulling away from her sisters, who stood startled by her words. "Pikkaq's faith was in us. Would you, through flabby tongues, have her loss a waste?"

With these last few words, Tuki touched upon something shameful to Igutaapiit ears, for the Bee Folk could not stand the idea of waste. Tuki's sisters stood silent for a long moment, before one of them said, "You shame us, Tuki. But what can we do?"

"I don't know," Tuki answered. "What are we here for?"

"Pikkaq knew most of it," the second sister said. "But I know there's a sacred thing. In Taqqiq's custody."

"This was to be a contest," the first sister said. "Taqqiq was to hand over the sacred thing. To whichever folk won."

"And that's why we're guests, here?" Tuki guessed. "We're competing against the other guests, for this . . . thing?"

Tuki's sisters droned in the affirmative.

"We must compete," Tuki told them. "We must make Taqqiq allow us that. At least we'll show that our kind cannot be stepped upon. Cannot be ignored. Cannot be broken."

Tuki's sisters droned in the affirmative.

It took time for the sisters to jostle their way toward the silver fire, shoving aside guests that hopped, hooted, undulated, and shrieked. They wound their way through the thickening crowd in order to avoid those guests it seemed unwise to touch (such as a being whose flesh churned like liquid embers, and another whose limbs warned with razors of quartz).

Tuki, all the while, restrained her questions about the strange flame toward which they struggled, though it seemed logical, to her, to suppose that the flame represented the one who had invited all: Taqqiq himself. By the time the Bee sisters were almost upon it, Tuki could hear voices sissing, snapping, graunching around her. Something had stimulated the guests, for many were turning to one another, issuing statements such as:

"Taqqiq has decided!"

"It's going to the Naaraajik!"

"The Abdominous One has it!"

Tuki had no idea what all this buzzing meant, though she guessed that it might not bode well for the Igutaapiit mission. And she found herself struggling to care about the mission, for she'd never had much of its purpose explained to her. She was conscious of but one fact: she would not allow that Pikkaq had died in vain.

At last, the sisters broke through the crowd and into an open circle, around which towered the marble antlers they'd seen at a distance. At the far side of the ring, floating almost as high as the pointed heights of the antlers themselves, there knelt a man. He might have easily been mistaken for one of the Human Folk, given his general form; but his eyes seemed more akin to openings, rather than organs of sight, offering slit glimpses into a burning white core. The man's hair snaked like silvern rivers about his shoulders, ever curling, recombining with his seat of living Moon-fire. Even the decorative clothes upon his body, articles that Tuki had seen Human Folk sew from hides of animals, seemed to spangle and coruscate, as though laced with captured light.

Bobbing but slightly in the air, the man knelt at the heart of the grand silver flame. He was bathed in its light and, Tuki sensed, at once generating it. Tuki required no special wisdom to realize that she now beheld the very innua of the Moon, its lord and master dreamer: Taqqiq himself.

As Tuki stared, Taqqiq inclined his head slightly, so that the cold fire of his gaze seemed to fall upon Tuki and her sisters. For a moment, Tuki felt the strangeness of Taqqiq's thoughts brush up against her own, a breath-stealing influence like the sudden embrace of tide. Yet unlike Aagjuk, the singing crone, Taqqiq's will seemed to carry a scent of self-restraint, as though the being knew that even his errant thoughts, his unfettered whimsies, might damage the minds of his guests. Still, there returned, in the moment when Tuki's and Taqqiq's eyes met, the notion Tuki had earlier experienced in meeting Aagjuk's gaze: that there was no man here, just as there was no silver flame. Tuki looked only upon symbols, representing some incomprehensible power in the Moon itself.

Then Taqqiq rubbed at his temples, like a man in the grip of a headache. His gaze returned to the centre of the open floor, and Tuki's mind was released from the tidal force of the A'aa's awareness. For the first time since Tuki and her sisters had made it to the circle's edge, she noticed all that stood before her.

She could barely believe that she had overlooked it:

A great, gelatinous hulk dominated the floor's centre, shuddering and throbbing at several times the stature of many encircling guests. At first, it seemed to Tuki that she beheld a small mountain of mud, or jelly, or excrement, or perhaps some rancid midden of all such things. But she quickly realized that the monstrosity was vaguely spherical, owning simple, almost foetal limbs, numbering four in total. Crowning its bulk, as though plastered in place via crudest clay-work, was the travesty of a head, holding two bulbous eyes. But for the lack of gills, it reminded Tuki of fish she had seen: perhaps a cod.

It seemed, upon first glance, that the odious creature possessed skin that shifted, squirming of its own accord. But Tuki saw, after a moment, that there was no skin. The strange being was truly akin to muddied jelly. Here and there, where the dirt permitted, Tuki could see that the creature was porous, pocked with thousandfold holes where sea-like worms burrowed and slid and feasted. In many places across its moist surface, nematodes emerged with their many legs and nipping jaws to do battle against lice as large as Tuki's fist. At once, many other vermin, less recognizable, skittered and picked their way across the gelatinous landscape. Sometimes, they fell upon one another in an orgy of death and cannibalism; at other times, they dropped eggs.

Then Taqqiq, hovering above all, spoke with a strangely muted voice, like someone uttering words through a rag. Still, the voice was somehow penetrating, despite its odd quality, and Tuki realized that it blew like a breeze across her very wits. It spoke without true sound, as though its words were Tuki's own. In this way, while the A'aa's lips were motionless, the Moon Lord nevertheless stated:

"With no further challengers, I declare the contest finished. The Naaraajik has proven his hunger competent to meet the prize."

"We challenge!" the sisters of the Bee Folk cried out nearly as one. "We, Igutaapiit! We, Animal Folk!"

The general babel of the strange guests fell to low hissing and whispers, as the great hulk in the centre of the area planted all four limbs, then raised itself from the floor. There followed a hideous stench, from which many of the guests reeled, as though something rancid had met the air. The jellied horror's head seemed to melt into its body, as though the creature were consuming itself. But after a long moment, in which guests and Bee sisters composed themselves in the wake of the fetor, the same head emerged from the creature's bottom half. Those bulbous eyes, not so much opening as growing from the thing's head, came to regard the Bee sisters.

"Not fair!" the creature belched. "Not fair, Taqqiq! You made a ruling. The loathsome Animal Folk could have taken up my challenge earlier."

"There is some justice to that," Taqqiq soughed into the wits of all present. "Do you have an answer, representatives of the Animal Folk? Of all your kind, you were the only ones to accept my invitation. So it is reasonable to suppose that you may answer for yourselves."

"We were delayed," one of the Bee warriors answered after a moment.

"But we're here, now," another Bee warrior added.

"We're blind and lost," Tuki contributed in all honesty, "by the loss of our leader. She was fearless, but she fell along the way. And, I'm sorry for our rudeness, but we will not let her die in vain."

The other Bee sisters droned their displeasure at Tuki's words, perhaps embarrassed that Tuki had made public knowledge of their travails.

Taqqiq's smile was grim, and he again rubbed at his temples. "Aagjuk goes too far at times," he said in his soundless way, "but she is one of the laws governing the Moon, and I would create disorder by blocking her ways. Ask no more about this. I am sorry for your loss, Animal Folk. But did you not know to ignore her antics?"

Tuki, who had been the sole weakling to fall before Aagjuk's test of wills, fidgeted with shame.

"I will extend the challenge," Taqqiq went on. "Or, rather, the Naaraajik's challenge," he added, indicating the four-legged abomination at centre floor, "since it is his kind who have issued it. The Abdominous Ones have claimed to be able to consume anything. All you must do is prove them wrong."

"Let us end the foolishness, Taqqiq," the Naaraajik croaked, still eyeing the Igutaapiit sisters. "I have eaten for hours, today, but I have eaten for entire cycles of the Moon at times when I am not in play. This has all been a wonderful game, but how many boulders, burning coals, pillars of ice, acids, poisons, talismans, furniture, pets, and other tedious things will I be required to swallow? I grow bored."

Tuki was taken aback by the Abdominous One's words. How long had this contest been going on? Had challengers really thrown such things at the Naaraajik—and had they all been consumed?

"Devour this!" one of the Bee sisters cried; and she hurled her weapon, a rippling levin spear, at the Naaraajik.

Tuki stiffened with alarm at her sister's boldness. Though she did not know why, Tuki was nagged by the feeling that there was a trick here. The usual Igutaapiit directness invited only catastrophe.

As fast as the Strong spear flew, the Abdominous One's mouth seemed to open faster. A slit, great and dark and blending the creature's mouth to its body, seemed to open without true movement. In one beat of the heart, the mouth seemed to loom, vast as the night sky itself, to encompass the spear's tiny lightning flash. Tuki watched the Igutaapiit weapon, among the fiercest of tools in any Animal Folk arsenal, wink out into the Naaraajik's depths, as though its very light had been guttled down. Then the hideous mouth was closed.

The Naaraajik chortled, seating itself with a small explosion of moisture and pulverized vermin, as the Bee sisters stood aghast. Next to Tuki, the other Bee sister (she who had not yet tried her weapons, which were alike to Tuki's own) seemed to shake with rage.

As for Tuki herself, she felt strangely detached from the events before her, as though her mind were adrift and rebellious. A sort of song seemed to arise almost to consciousness, teasing from the well of her being. Dimly, she wondered if the happenings on the Moon had finally driven her mad. Why could she not focus? Why could she not be like the rest of her sisters, and take the direct path?

The Abdominous One continued to laugh, taking a moment to scrape up a handful of its own struggling vermin, which it downed in a swallow.

Before Tuki or the other Bee sister could stop her, the enraged sister rushed forward, blades flashing. Tuki cried out a warning—but not in time to prevent the Abdominous One from rolling forward, moving with dread fleetness despite its size. The mouth opened, its inner murk seeming to somehow draw the lone Bee sister in, then snapped closed. It had moved with such speed that she had not even managed to strike a blow.

Tuki and her remaining sister cried out, and Tuki dropped her blades. The weapons tinkled like crystal shards on the pearly floor.

"You see?" the Naaraajik belched, its head coming around to look up at Taqqiq. "Their little stings only mean more food for me. None have met my challenge, Taqqiq. Give me the prize, Moon Dreamer. I will devour it now, and leave this place, for I can no longer stand the stuff of your imaginings beneath my feet."

Tuki, however, barely heard the Naaraajik's voice. A part of her had locked itself into purest despair, even while another voice seemed to breathe words across her mind. Aagjuk's song arose, then, the few words Tuki had heard of a sudden abloom in her consciousness. And she remembered:

Who will have the ones unwanted?
The voids that know but lonely spark.
As well to guttle down the world,
And make of dream unending drink . . .

The place where every guest now stood, Tuki realized, was Taqqiq's dream—was it not? They stood as guests not only in the Moon Lord's abode, but also in his mind.

"Eat the floor," Tuki called out to the Naaraajik.

The Abdominous One froze, its head coming about some-where between Tuki and Taqqiq. "That is a ridiculous request," the Naaraajik said. "If there are no more *items* offered to meet my appetite, I claim victory, Taqqiq."

"Eat this place," Tuki demanded.

"Taqqiq," the Abdominous One whinged at the Moon Lord, "I demand my prize. I will not honour the absurdities of the filthy Animal Folk."

"Eat the Moon," Tuki pressed.

"Taqqiq," the Naaraajik continued, ignoring Tuki, "where is the prize?"

The Moon Master smiled, then, the silvern slits of his eyes narrowing. "Your challenge is met again, Naaraajik," said Taqqiq. "Is it that you have misspoken? Can it be that your kind cannot devour all things? The floor beneath you is real, but only because I will it so. And I am eternal. Therefore, my will is ever-during. You have eaten for hours, today, yes. And we have all witnessed that the boasts of your kind are not without foundation. But it remains for you to ask yourself: Would you test a river without source? A well without bottom? I am not sure, myself. You are Strong, and perhaps you will devour even my abode, and therefore my essence along with it. But have no fear for your prize. I leave it before you, so that if I disappear, you may at least claim it."

The eyes of the Moon Lord closed, like twin lamp flames winking out. The very air seemed to shudder, then, as though it had become dense as water, and Tuki's balance became uncertain. Tuki stumbled somewhat, along with the other guests, though all managed to keep their footing. When the fleeting strangeness passed, Taqqiq's eyes were again open, directed at something on the floor:

Next to the Naaraajik, there sat an egg. It was a large egg, perhaps as big as Tuki's head, and across its surface surged whorls of alternating blue and white, as though it were enwreathed with shallow storm.

Many of the assembled guests, including the Naaraajik, gasped at the sight of the egg, though it meant nothing to Tuki.

"Behold the *Hilaup Manninga*," Taqqiq announced with great gravity, "your prize, Naaraajik. Should you succeed. I have arranged that, should you devour all before you, including myself, the egg will yet fall into your custody. Ask no more about this. It is time to prove your boasts."

The Naaraajik seemed to shudder upon sight of the egg, though Tuki realized, after a moment, that the reaction was not one of awe, but of lust. Already, in eyeing the strange egg, the Naaraajik's mouth seemed to open of its own accord. Many of the vermin across the Abdominous One's surface began to dig, as though to shelter themselves in the gelatinous flesh.

The Naaraajik seemed to pull its gaze away from the egg only with great effort. Then it came to eye Taqqiq, then Tuki, then the floor. Upon the floor it at last held its gaze, long and unblinking, before Tuki saw the great mouth stretching. It moved slowly, this time, as though the appetite impelling it were reticent. Tuki watched the black slit widen, expanding across the lower third of the Naaraajik's head, before it went on across the Abdominous One's body. The blackness within that maw seemed somehow more complete than any mere lack of light, as though beyond the mind's ability to conceive of darkness, and Tuki found herself having to avert eyes from it.

Then the Abdominous One rolled. With mouth to the floor, it began to eat.

A strange shiver ran through the hall, causing many of the guests to cry out in fear. Tuki, as one of the Igutaapiit, could not share in their terror, but she nevertheless experienced a pang of alarm, wondering if the Naaraajik might actually succeed in devouring Taqqiq's hall, Taqqiq's very mind, and all it contained.

"I dislike words," Tuki's sister muttered at her side. "But if we die here, I want you to know. I do not think little of you, sister. In all of us, Pikkaq would have been proud."

Tuki droned in pleasure, reaching down to pick up her blades. She handed one of them to her sister, whose spear had been consumed by the Naaraajik. If it came to death, neither of them would venture into the next world with empty hands.

Then all alarm drained out of Tuki—for she glanced upward, and saw Taqqiq, floating upon his seat of flame.

She saw that the Moon Lord was smiling.

Tuki's eyes then flickered to the Naaraajik; and she became aware of whines interspersed among the sucking noises of the Abdominous One's feast. The Naaraajik of a sudden seemed to weep as it ate, its great mouth having by now stretched across its

entire form, dividing it almost in half. The creature lay pressed
and prone upon the nacre of Taqqiq's floor, as though having tried
to encompass the surface in one grand kiss. And it seemed to Tuki
that the floor somehow kissed back, rising and becoming one with
the embrace of the Naaraajik's mouth, so that it had captured the
creature's very flesh. While the Naaraajik shivered and moaned,
the devourer's bulk seemed to recede into the pearlescent surface,
until even the vermin at last abandoned their jellied home, moving outward in waves from the centre of the floor. As the vermin
went among the circle of guests, most were trampled underfoot
(with some being caught by the odder guests, by whom they were
devoured).

The Naaraajik, Tuki understood, was murdering itself upon
the endless dreams of Taqqiq. By that alchemy born of admixed
ignorance and arrogance, the Naaraajik had sought to consume a
force without true substance: the very will of the Moon. By those
strange laws in which the Strength of things ebbed and flowed, the
force of the Naaraajik's hunger had become reversed. In attempt-
ing to eat all, it ate but one:

Itself.

"Stop!" Tuki cried, feeling a sort of panic come over her. She
realized, after a moment, that it was compassion for the Naaraajik.

"Stop!" she repeated.

The Abdominous One's eyes rolled madly, only one of the
orbs coming to settle on Tuki. Still, the feeding went on, the
Naaraajik melding into the floor with each passing moment. The
creature was, by now, but a third of its original size.

Overhead, Taqqiq was laughing.

"A waste," Tuki's sister hissed at her side. She shifted her
blade from one hand to the other, shaking her head at the spec-
tacle.

"A waste," Tuki agreed. The Igutaapiit had no love of need-
less death.

Of a sudden, the Naaraajik drew in what remained of itself. It reared back from the floor with a heaving cry as of many lungs in concert. By now, the Naaraajik had somehow consumed its own limbs, even its own eyes, so that it had become a quivering spire of gelatinous filth, cut across by a void-filled slash. As the wreck of the creature bobbed to left and right, its mouth issued another long cry, wracked and despairing.

Without warning, the Naaraajik rolled, pouring itself like a wave of grease upon the egg. The edges of that mouth, which had snatched up one of Tuki's sisters before she had managed to so much as strike at it, flashed outward like the beat of black wings. None of the assembled guests, nor Tuki herself, had time to even gasp at the sudden action. The Naaraajik, it seemed, had simply stolen its prize.

The Moon Lord, however, was faster. Taqqiq raised only his chin, and silvern fire engulfed the Naaraajik. Tuki watched as the Moon Master clenched his left fist, and the flames surged into an argent storm. The living pyre was strangely without heat or sound, though it was blinding, and it left the mind giddy and fey. Like many of the guests, Tuki was forced to turn away from it.

Tuki soon after felt her sister's touch, and her voice saying: "Sister, look."

Tuki turned back to the Naaraajik and saw that the flame of Taqqiq had turned it white, like salt or ash. The fleetness of the Moon Lord's wrath had been such that the Naaraajik now seemed like a statue, curving over its prize, its amorphous lips almost upon the eggshell. As for the egg itself, it sat under the calcine Naaraajik, unmarred.

Taqqiq clapped once, and the remains of the Naaraajik collapsed, becoming a great blanket of ash across the open floor.

Taqqiq smiled down upon Tuki and her sister, then regarded the assembled guests. "Of all the peoples I have invited to meet the Naaraajik's challenge," the great Agony announced, "only these Animal Folk—"

"Igutaapiit," Tuki interjected.

"Igutaapiit," her sister repeated.

"Very well," Taqqiq went on, still smiling, "Igutaapiit. Only these have met the challenge of the Abdominous One. They have therefore proven their will superior to the hunger of that one's kind. The Hilaup Manninga will endure, then, rather than knowing obliteration. It will endure under the guardianship of the Igutaapiit."

Taqqiq gestured toward the egg, now pale with a dusting of the Naaraajik's ash. "Please," the Agony said to Tuki and her sister, "take it, and let your Elders decide how it is to be treated. I will provide you with safe passage back to your home, should you decide you have tired of the wonders of my own." The Moon Lord rubbed at his temples again. "Now," he added, "this has made a day of length and bother. Let us all rest."

While Tuki's sister strode forward, kicking ash aside, and moving to claim the egg, Tuki herself stood staring at Taqqiq. Even as she felt the guests dispersing around her (though they were careful not to jostle her out of newfound respect), Tuki remained rooted.

"What has transpired today?" she thought at the Moon Master. He might choose not to respond, she knew, but nothing might convince her that he could not hear.

Taqqiq sat hunched amid his curling silver, of a sudden looking very tired. Then, projecting in a new and deeper way, like a voice whispering in a tightly enclosed space—a way that Tuki sensed was for her mind alone—Taqqiq told her:

"An outcome has been chosen, today, that will echo into all the Strong places, Bee warrior."

"Chosen?" Tuki thought back at the Moon Lord.

"Of course. All things are choice. Did you not choose, Tuki, to disregard all advice? To listen to the song of Aagjuk?"

Tuki was taken aback for a moment, but then sent:

"So you know about that. Then you also know this all means

nothing to me. I acted for the honour of my folk. Of my leader, Pikkaq, who did not have to die in that way."

Taqqiq issued a light laugh. "Pikkaq," he sent, "was wise. Wise enough to know that it should not be herself who faced the Naaraajik. Did you not know that it was why she chose you to accompany her here? We discussed it at length."

"You discussed it?" Tuki sent, at once horrified and confused.

"Naturally," Taqqiq sent, a grave tone colouring his sending. "Sometimes, fate is too important to be left to fate. Only you, Tuki, possessed a certain quality that we felt would be needed here. You are not exactly like the rest of your folk. Or have you not noticed? There is too much of the innua in you, and it makes you more akin to those of the Human Folk. It was Aagjuk who first noted that."

"Aagjuk?" Tuki sent. "But she's mad. Evil."

"Only when she has to be," Taqqiq sent. "We have our parts to play, she and I. Even Singuuri. The laws of Strength like to mock us all. But ask no more about this. Are you not even going to pester me about the prize?"

"An egg," Tuki sent with derision. "I don't care."

"You should," Taqqiq returned. "It is among the rarest of things in all the Lands, high, low, wide, far, and near. It is no less than the Hilaup Manninga—an egg born of the very Sky. Not the sky that you think of when you look at stars, Tuki, but the vaster one. The secret Sky, which gives rise even to Strength. One day, something very important will be born of this egg."

Tuki made a chuffing noise. "Reversed and roundabout talk," she sent, trying to call upon that practicality of which the Bee Folk were so proud, though, in truth, she sensed some peculiar import in Taqqiq's words.

Again, Taqqiq smiled. "Perhaps," the Moon Lord sent, "you are more alike to your folk than Aagjuk thought. Or perhaps the facets of your nature are simply well balanced. Perhaps that is why you won against the Naaraajik, and why you have such responsibility ahead of you." The Moon Master sighed, rubbing at his temples. "Perhaps," he added, "it would have been better for you, Tuki, if the Naaraajik had simply devoured the egg."

Tuki made no reply, standing for a long moment, watching her sister cradle the egg in her arms.

"Or perhaps," Tuki at last sent back to the Moon Lord, "that might have been . . . a waste."

Taqqiq laughed and the flames about him curled inward across his form, until his grinning face was the last to be obscured by curling silver. Then the argent mass swirled, shrinking into a ball, growing ever tighter and brighter, as though it somehow radiated in upon itself.

And the Moon Lord was gone.

◦ ◦ ◦

In this way did the Igutaapiit, those fierce sisters of the Bee Folk, become the traditional guardians of the Hilaup Manninga. The egg was brought home to the Elders, who later met with other Elders of the Animal Folk; and by their collective wisdom, they discerned something of the prophecy surrounding that prize of the Moon. It was later said that the cracking of the Hilaup Manninga would either herald an age of dread for the Land, or ring in a new time of providence for all. Only the Bee Folk, however, best know the direction toward which the prophecy leans. The wisest among them speak of this no more than of the egg itself, which lies warm and guarded beneath their Hidden fastnesses. As for Tuki, she was no longer considered the least wise of her folk, though it is said that she did not stay among them for long after her return. Between the words of Taqqiq and the song of Aagjuk, an intrepid seed had come to burgeon within her breast. In wholly Human form, or so it is told, she left to sample those greater wonders of the Land.

And she did not consider them a waste.

THE WOLF
WIGHT'S DIRGE

He could feel the innua, the essence of all that was Human, slipping from him.

Like others of his camp, both kith and kin, its loss had become as a yawning chasm within him, an ice-crack beyond which lay a nameless state more forbidding than any chill and lightless water. For neither Ikumaniq, nor kith, nor kin, had ever fully owned their Humanity.

Certainly, whenever they had gone upon two legs in the past, they had worn clothes as did the Humankind; and their ways had included the Human ways of speech, the wielding of tools, even of ceremony and song. Yet they had never forgotten that other half of themselves, and their best songs were of their origins in the eldritch times, the *Taissumani*, before Humankind had labelled itself "Inhabitant," others "animal." In those nascent days, two-legged and four-legged had exchanged skins as readily as knowledge, uttering one tongue between Sky and Land. So had it been, and a fine remembrance at that, but it was today no more than remembrance, and rarely did Humankind any longer recognize wisdom in either beast or bird. Too many times had arrogant Human Folk tried to make guests of themselves in Ikumaniq's camp, counting upon the Human custom of each camp welcoming travellers from another. It was only the ones of vision, those Some Seen, who balked and turned their sleds away at the last minute, seeing the truth of Ikumaniq's camp. For, whether kith or kin, every soul that Ikumaniq had ever loved was as himself: *Amaruq Inuruqsimajuq*, a Wolf who knew Human form.

Now, Ikumaniq rubbed at his eyes, pressing, as though he might dig fingers into them. It was something he did to draw his mind away from the rising sense of smell that threatened to whelm him utterly. There were scents in the air, of a sudden as solid as tent or tool, searing as flame or bitter cold. As the innua, the Humanity, seemed tenuous within him, so it left only his *uumaniq*—the rawest, most vulgar stuff of animal life. He cried out, then, loosing something like a canine yip rather than a Human wail, before his sister, Puajuq, distracted him with a hand upon his shoulder.

Ikumaniq wheeled, opening his eyes, repressing a snarl, and he regarded his sister. At this moment, Puajuq's face was only half of Wolf, her fully furred throat bunching out over the base of her hood, like some absurd white collar. A pointed ear rode high upon her head, separating raven locks, while the other ear had chosen to stay Human. Her upper teeth and lip were those of a Wolf, refusing to mesh with a still-Human lower jaw, and Ikumaniq sensed that she could not speak. Her widened eyes instead—welling as much with terror as pity—conveyed a weak concern for Ikumaniq. They were all suffering in the same way, the loss of their innua striking as might some disease among a Human encampment.

Ikumaniq forced a smile for his sister, his lips Human enough for the moment. Then he turned to regard the rest of the camp. It was early spring, so that sun shone upon ice and snow like auric fire, and Ikumaniq stifled a sob at the thought of what joy such weather might have brought him on any other day. Now, his folk staggered like mad souls from *iglu* dome to dome, groaning, weeping, panting, even growling as the feral state seized their throats. No individual was alike to another, for the innua withered against the uumaniq of each in a unique way, never remaining either patterned or lasting. Even as Ikumaniq turned, his right arm was lost, in an instant nearly all white and lupine up to the shoulder. It would most likely return in the next moment, though he knew one thing for certain: his arm would lose something of the Humanness that it had possessed before, as though each change were a dip in strange water, washing away only the two-legged part of his nature.

"Why?" Puajuq asked. The upper half of her head was wholly Wolf, though her mouth had at least become Human enough to speak with.

"Qissirtuq," Ikumaniq managed to say, citing the name of his closest male friend. Qissirtuq, along with three other of the camp's finest pursuers and trackers, had left before sunrise, using their personal Strength to track the pseudo-scent of their innua on the wind. All could feel that the innua was yet out there, somewhere, but few would speak of their greatest fear: that their most dire enemies, the *Nanurlualuit*, had found some black means by which to prey upon it.

Ikumaniq shook his head, suddenly unable to pronounce further words, and he suppressed a howl as his back became bent, as if trying to force him closer to the earth. But it was at least a distraction from his sister, who, panicking, kept pressing him about the lost innua—as though he possessed more knowledge than she. He knew that it was because he had been out hunting. The morning had seen many of the Amaruit Inuruqsimajuit on the hunt. As always occurred at such times, each hunter had put aside Humanity in order to go upon the swifter four legs instead of two. Since time immemorial, such had been their way, so that sedentary existence saw them in skin of Human, the chase in fell of Wolf. Fully as Wolves had they enjoyed their shining day (for while Wolves respect the moon, the wise know that they best love the sun), and they had experienced nothing unusual either on the way out or the way back.

Something, however, *had* gone wrong. As with most hunts, the Amaruq Inuruqsimajuq had returned, bloody, jostling, satisfied, gathering, and greeting in the centre of the camp. Each had then reached out to his or her own portion of the camp's innua, awaiting the return to uprightness, to cool skin and grasping hands and blunted scent. Yet the innua had come as but a trickle, like droplets from a water-skin that has gone damaged and unnoticed until raised to dry lips. Then had come the terror, like windblown sparks among their spirits, each sucking at his dregs of innua like lungs at rarefied air, for while they had often made mock of their Humanness, they knew that they were but simple wolves without it. Each had scavenged enough, then, to regain something of the Human semblance; but since that time the affliction had spread to even those who had not gone hunting, and the remaining innua was at wane.

Everyone could sense that the heart of the communal innua was gone—perhaps somehow misplaced, probably stolen. But how could a thief, even a Some Seen one, grasp such essence in order to make away with it? If the dread Nanurlualuit had somehow managed to do this, it was by a new craft of Strength foreign to Ikumaniq's folk. If anyone were to know, it should have been the Grand Mother, eldest and most beloved of the Amaruit Inuruqsimajuit, who knew the Strength of the Land's deepest veins. Once, she had seemed invulnerable, of overarching pomp. Rarely did she reveal herself on even the most important of occasions. Now, she was entirely cloistered in the small iglu which Ikumaniq himself had built for her months ago, ashamed to show herself. For it was said that she suffered even worse than others the loss of her innua, and did not wish to appear as abominable before the eyes of her folk.

With a hand brandishing more claws than fingernails, Puajuq again touched Ikumaniq, drawing his attention to some commotion at the edge of camp. Ikumaniq followed her, then, stumbling upon incompatible legs until he had joined the small crowd. Approaching his kith and kin from behind, seeing the lot of them in their pitiable states, was like viewing the community through thin ice or quartz. Almost all were in constant transition, now, with mismatched body parts streaming like fast smoke or mirages; and no single part, whether Human or Wolf, remained steady for long. From a lone Human eye, Ikumaniq's tears trailed down across white-furred cheek, and he shivered; and while the chill of the Land had never before concerned him, his very heart now seemed mantled with ice.

"We have tracked it!" cried a voice ahead of the crowd. After a moment, Ikumaniq recognized it as belonging to Qissirtuq, his good friend. Qissirtuq and his three companion trackers had finally returned. As the last of them—Qissirtuq's smoke-coloured wife, Tununiq—loped into the camp, Ikumaniq could see that all were unwell. They had gone out upon four legs, but had barely been able to enter camp upon the traditional two, so that their upper halves retained some semblance of Human form, while their lower legs remained canine. With few words, as though eager to spare them shame, camp folk passed them clothing and the trackers hurriedly donned whatever they were handed. Many pretended not to see when Qissirtuq failed to keep the boots upon his canine legs.

"Where?" asked Ikumaniq, echoing the cries of many of those gathered. Qissirtuq saw him and smiled, robust features mostly Human for the moment. The friends did not touch in greeting, however, for they were in form loathsome to one another.

"Stolen," Qissirtuq replied, "by Humankind."

There were hisses and growls, all around, in response to this revelation. Ikumaniq heard his sister's voice behind him cry out:

"Too long have we suffered nearness to those of one skin! To the Humankind!" Her words were echoed by many, and Ikumaniq himself nodded in agreement with the sentiment. Humankind! It was not insulting enough, it seemed, that they flaunted their innua—given to them freely and without bounds by Creation—but now they were stealing it from the four-legged folk!

"We should ravage their camps!" Puajuq went on. "Retake our innua! And blood for equal measure!"

"Beware," Ikumaniq said in a low snarl at his sister, speaking only with difficulty. "All Animal Folk forbid such words. Folk of beast, folk of bird—none take Human."

"Prey is prey," Puajuq insisted.

"Murder," Ikumaniq said, though he only muttered the word, doubting his own argument. It had often seemed ridiculous to him that Human Folk remained exempt from the hunt.

With some urgency in his tone, Qissirtuq was speaking again, and quickly. He explained to all that the lost innua lay in no Human camp, but had instead been traced to a tiny and nearby shelter of snow, not unlike the sort of den carved out upon snowy slopes by the mothering white bears. All of the assembled Amaruit Inuruqsimajuit were amazed when they heard this, demanding to know how their innua had fallen into such a place, and what this could mean.

"None can tell," Qissirtuq answered, for the moment more Wolf than man. "But when we stood listening, we heard cries from that shelter. Cries as of Human infants."

"Humankind!" several voices snarled. Ikumaniq's was among them, for he was incensed that Human Folk had indeed been responsible for the theft of innua. At once, however, he wondered why Human infants would occupy a snow shelter.

"And did you not rip them from that place?" a harsh and

strident voice pressed. Again, it was Puajuq.

When Qissirtuq tried to answer, a strained canine sound emerged, so that he snapped his maw closed. In his shame, he looked away from the crowd.

"We fled that place," Qissirtuq's wife went on in her husband's stead, although Tununiq's own words were nearly mangled in her throat. There were instant snarls of admonition in response to what many (including Ikumaniq) perceived to be cowardice on the part of the trackers, and some shot forward, snapping despite Tununiq's high rank. But the smoky Tununiq bared her own fangs, unflinching, and cried:

"Away, dogs, so that I may speak! The Nanurlualuit came! They have scented the innua upon winds of Strength. And would devour it for themselves."

An instant dolour fell over the camp, the shock of hearing the very name of their enemies enough to invoke silence. But for the incessant changes in form, as though each camp dweller were ever being turned in some warped lens, there was stillness. The chill had extended itself to Ikumaniq's bowels.

"That is why we return," Tununiq explained. "Between Strength and swiftness does our innua now survive."

No further explanation, however, had been required of Qissirtuq's wife. Already, more than half of the assembled Amaruit Inuruqsimajuit were setting aside what little of their Humanness they now possessed, bodies shimmering as of sun upon water, limbs as a whorl of snow caught at the edge of vision. The Strength of the Land swept through them all, usually so welcome, but now become a thing of dread. For Ikumaniq, like his kith and kin, knew that the fragile remaining traces of innua would only erode with each exchange of skin. Even now, he could feel the unbalanced uumaniq looming within him—the pure Wolf waiting to devour his mind.

Now upon the Wolf's four legs, Ikumaniq's attention turned toward his sister. Perceiving the scent of her first, the sight of her almost an afterthought, he noticed that she yet went up-right.

"I . . . cannot," she apologized. "What if there is none left, after?"

Ikumaniq bared his teeth, disgusted at his sibling's fear of losing her last shred of innua; then he wheeled from her, joining the others who were already at a run, having left the camp to follow Qissirtuq.

For nigh unto an hour did the pack—almost two dozen Amaruit Inuruqsimajuit—run with all speed, before the sun at last seemed smothered within folds of grey and tangled clouds. All knew that it meant driving snow; and with the knowledge came fear, for their foes had ever exulted in the embrace of storm.

Another hour followed, the only sounds in Ikumaniq's ears those of his panting, over the vague hiss of many claws upon ice. Then, when the blizzard fell like dark wings about them, so that Ikumaniq could sense most of his company by scent alone, Qissirtuq threw thoughts upon the wind. In this silent way, ancient beyond speech, he directed Ikumaniq to run with those who went left and rearward, while he himself took others to the right.

As ever, as in the hunt, Ikumaniq obeyed without hesitation, though the storm was thickening, and he could barely see the tail of Qissirtuq's wife ahead of him.

Moments later, Ikumaniq quailed, skidding to a halt; for the scent of Qissirtuq's thoughts had faded and there now came upon Ikumaniq a great blight of mind, vast and grasping, like a pit delved in the Land's own Strength. Ikumaniq trembled, then, for he knew that his spirit had sampled the will of the enemy. It was near, and the Nanurlualuit were so confident as to make no effort at concealing themselves.

There was a yip from somewhere ahead, followed by the sense of Hidden sinews going taut, and Ikumaniq knew that one of his company had unleashed personal Strength. He snarled, fearing and hating all of Creation for a moment, before racing forward, seeking battle. Instead, he was met with a wave of attainted Strength, and the driven snow assumed sudden indigo hue, catching him up, kneading him like a gobbet of flesh rolled between a titan's palms. Ikumaniq was sent tumbling along unseen tides, unsure of his direction, before at last finding his feet in a desperate scramble. He rose, uneasy, with the feeling as of a foul dinner readying to leave the stomach, and he turned.

The lone Nanurlualuk emerged from shreds of storm, unhurried, vast, and terrible upon its four legs. Then it reared, going upon hind legs, so that Ikumaniq could well behold the travesty that chimera had made of a white bear's form. For while the Nanurlualuit all favoured the semblance of the bear, they were of an ilk at once Hidden and vile. The Nanurlualuk before Ikumaniq wore a bear's fell only as a pauper wears rags, and the lack of hair, as of rampant mange, showed more black skin than white fur across its form; a constant walk upon false paws had left the flesh about its feet to hang in yellowed tatters; and its hide gaped open in places, whether from wear or wound, the larger rents offering glimpses of mottled and glutinous motion beneath. This strange flesh of the Nanurlualuit, Ikumaniq remembered, shed a dire tar in its wake.

The bear chimera, still rearing, sniffed at the Hidden winds in order to probe Ikumaniq's Strength. It fixed no obvious gaze upon him, for its vision was sevenfold and not unalike to that of a spider, each tiny and onyx orb fixed upon the doings of an alternate world. In that moment, Ikumaniq forgot to cast his own regard away from the chimera's eyes, and the black orbs ensnared his mind, drawing his will and selfhood into the places where they ever stared. Ikumaniq knew, then, that he had fallen before even fighting, for he could hear sendings of the Nanurlualuk's mind as it gloated:

Falls a pitiful Wolf Wight . . .

But there was a cry to Ikumaniq's right, shattering the fugue about him, and he turned in time to see Tununiq, Qissirtuq's

smoke-coloured wife, in the fullness of her Strength. She had shed her four-legged form, now standing as mingled Wolf and woman, white-furred fists upraised. And it seemed, for an instant, that Ikumaniq beheld a lambent river flowing upward from the Land at her feet, and that she was one with that Strength, so that it curved through her and out between her fists. And that power, inherent to Creation (however ancient and strange even to Amaruit Inuruqsimajuit), struck at the Nanurlualuk in a hail of light, akin to the flanks of many fish under summer sun.

The bear chimera loosed a terrible cry, shuddering and cavernous, then fell upon its front paws. At once, it opened its maw, within which Nanurlualuit bore their true and secret eyes, and it gazed upon Qissirtuq's wife.

Ikumaniq, near paralysed with terror, mustered all of his will in order to avoid the Nanurlualuk's inner eyes, and it was for this reason that he did not see the chimera's fall. Instead, he heard the Nanurlualuk cry out once again, then again, each utterance more despairing than the next. As well, there were flashes as of multi-hued flames all about him and the sense of his own kind merging their Strength. Yet Ikumaniq, having made something of a ball of himself, would not look up until all fell silent.

When Ikumaniq next looked about him, it was in wonder at the sound of sobbing. He then saw Qissirtuq, who had tried to assume two legs, but whose form was now little better than that of a deformed Wolf. It was Qissirtuq who was sobbing, and while he did so, he held his wife, rocking, with what arms he could manage. Tununiq was aflame, but with a hideous saffron fire that neither blackened nor withered; her eyes were wide, streaming tears, though there was nothing of awareness in them. Her *isuma*, Ikumaniq knew—her very selfhood—remained entrapped in that place were the true Nanurlualuit eyes ever dwelt, whether live or dead. Her mind would never return to the Land.

As for the enemy, the Strength-wrought storm was now thinning, and Ikumaniq could see that his kith and kin had prevailed. A great mound of something like ash or snow, though truly neither, now lay where Ikumaniq's attacker had fallen. Other such mounds sprawled here and there, wind-blown, and the Amaruit Inuruqsimajuit walked among them, most yet four-legged, tongues lolling in exhaustion. Their numbers had thinned and the Nanurlualuit had left little more than offal to mark the fallen.

Already, some few Amaruit Inuruqsimajuit were gathered near the shallow slope of a snow-covered hill. Ikumaniq was not close enough to see, though he could still sample the Hidden winds, and knew that the scent of powerful innua was there. For a moment, he thought about trying to catch Qissirtuq's attention, to ask if he were sensing the Human Folk in the shelter that the trackers had spoken of. But Qissirtuq had become useless, preoccupied with mourning his wife, and therefore as fallen, in battle, as she. Life, it seemed to Ikumaniq, was for those who might live it—and so he left them.

The absence of innua was now akin to starvation. Ikumaniq could think of little other than the need for that Human essence. All sentiment, all kinship, might wither before that hunger.

Ikumaniq joined the rest of his company, forming a half-circle near the base of the slope. The storm had expired with those bear chimeras that had drawn it, and the golden sun began to wink forth amid high, racing clouds. Even distant sight was again possible, and Ikumaniq could see that there was indeed a lone dark patch upon the slope above: a shelter. The innua seemed to waft from that place, at once pungent and delicious, as of blood upon the breeze.

Then, gathered in silence with the others, Ikumaniq could hear:

Infants—the distinct sounds of infants crying. And those throats were unmistakably Human.

There had to be a mother present, then. Perhaps a father. Some small family that had taken shelter, whether against storm or chimera.

After stealing the innua. And, upon this thought, Ikumaniq's rage pulled the lips back from his fangs.

"Come forth!" one of the company called. Similar voices, raw-edged, guttural, soon followed, each demanding:

"Emerge!"

"Face us, thieves!"

"Come, or we'll dig for you!"

There was movement near the lip of the shelter—a whiteness against the white, it seemed—as though something very small and wan had crawled forth. The company went silent, seeking with eyes and noses, even the Hidden senses, until it became apparent that there were two tiny creatures up there.

But they were not Human.

Ikumaniq paced, as amazed as the rest of his kith and kin, realizing that two white Wolf pups had emerged from the shelter. The pair at first seemed more preoccupied with each other than anything else, but eventually noticed Ikumaniq's company. Then the pups stiffened, staring down the snowy slope, backing with nervous fits and starts into the shelter again. The sun cast its gold across the slope, in that moment, drawing long shadows from the pups, and Ikumaniq realized that they were no simple wolves. The innua surrounded their frail forms with such Strength that it seemed as if unseen wings beat about them.

Then there came a longer shadow from the den, hunched at first, emerging to take up the pups each to an arm. The figure stood, after that, no longer a shadow, but revealed in full. It was, the company saw, their own Grand Mother—yet she stood without the least trace of Wolf about her, rather entirely in her Humanness. Her skin shone beneath the sun, so that the intricate tattoos were visible across her features; and while the patterns, like she herself, were old beyond reckoning, her face was young and beautiful to behold. Her regard, however, was stern.

A long silence followed, with only the sound of the wind about the company. In time, the unvoiced thoughts of all assembled came together as one, and a question hung as of something rank in the air:

Mother of Us All, have You taken our innua?

The Grand Mother seemed to sense the question, and her features softened, becoming sad.

"Long have I ceased to be Mother to you," she spoke aloud, with a voice as of dancing water, "for you have taken a path that I will not tread."

Ikumaniq snarled, then, along with many others, for he was realizing that she alone had been the thief of their innua. She alone had spared herself the suffering, the torment and shame and corruption into a simple beast's form, all the while that she had pretended to languish within her iglu.

The Grand Mother seemed to sense this thought, for she laughed without humour, a look of pain upon her face. Then she whispered something to the pups who sat, still as stones, in her arms. And there followed a blur, as of sunlight viewed through tears; and when Ikumaniq next saw clearly, there were no pups to be seen. There were, instead, infant twins—perfect in their Human-ness. The sight of them raised the hackles of the company, educing awe, for all of their kind lived upon four legs until adolescence, mastering two-legged existence only in young adulthood.

"I have begun my family anew," the Grand Mother said, glancing from one infant to another. "For my old are forsaken."

"Fiend!" Ikumaniq snarled, struggling as never before to summon voice. "Betrayer! Our innua stolen for these two?"

Balancing both infants, the Grand Mother wiped at tears, answering, "Do you yet not understand? It was you who forsook your innua. I cannot take such a thing from you, even by the Strength of the Land. Long have I watched you all, guided you in vain, while your ways have ever favoured Wolf over Human. There is but one nature that must rule, in the end. And my first family has chosen."

But even as the Grand Mother spoke, the company began

a steady stalk up the hillside, growls low in throat, eyes red and fixed, minds hinged upon murder. The Grand Mother, Ikumaniq dimly knew, had rendered herself useless, even dangerous. They would have back their innua, no matter the cost.

Then Ikumaniq's ears twitched about his head, for he was distracted by a strange and rising sound. And he realized, with a start, that it was singing. The Grand Mother stood with eyes closed, while the infant twins nestled close to her breast, and her voice issued out over the company like spreading water. Her tone was at once soothing and sad, as though she sang a dirge, and some few words of her eldritch dialect were alike to:

> *There dwelled a truth in weighted place,*
> *Where silent spirit, breast immured,*
> *Yet drove a cleansing wind secured,*
> *By the starlit wrought ashamed trace;*
> *Ere sunlit falsehood mastered word.*

The song seemed to stand outside of time, so that Ikumaniq was unsure of how long he listened, his mind a mist within which crept a miscellany of feelings, but little memorable thought.

Then, when the sun was low and the shadows quite long, he cast his gaze about, realizing that the woman on the hill had ceased in her noise. And he was very afraid, for he knew not where he stood, nor what to expect of this strange place. There were snarls and yips of pain behind him, also to his sides, and he turned to behold wolves. They were fetid with terror, with anger and confusion alike to his own, and had therefore set teeth to one another. Many others, he saw, had simply fled, so that the distant specks of them receded in several directions.

The wolf that had been Ikumaniq turned back to the slope one last time, noting the lingering Human scent, though there was now but a hole to view. Then he turned and fled: for the simple wolf, as with his kith, as with his kin, was all that was left to him.

SLIPPERY BABIES

It was late in that moon time of *Katagaarivik*, the "Time of Dropping," when the bull caribou have finished with their bloody jousts and antlers have fallen from heads till next season. It was also the time of winter's deep dark, when each day passed without sight of the sun.

Pilaaq wished that her mother would visit.

She nestled deeper into her bed: a sleeping pallet of many piled caribou hides, where she could feel her own heat admixed with the strange sting of chilled sweat. Sometimes, in frustration, she threw the blankets from herself, even rose from bed to wander about the tent on bare knees and hands. She never got far, at these times, since her husband always seemed to sense when she had crawled too far out of bed. Then there were unusual flapping sounds near the mouth of the tent—the layers her husband claimed to have placed in order to thoroughly block the wind—and the innermost flap would stir. Her husband would come rushing in to coo at her, after that, to stroke her hair, to gently butt at her with shoulders and hips, until she returned to bed.

"Look at the sweat pouring from you," he muttered after one of these times.

"I want my mother," she told him, perhaps for the hundredth time. Or had she ever voiced the demand at all? It was so hard to tell. Dream, reality—of late, she wove in and out of either awareness like a needle through sealskin.

"She'll come for you," her husband said in a gentle whisper. "You're still sick. You need to respect the care of others. It is a mother's duty to care. No one wants to disturb you."

Pilaaq did not answer for a moment, but then she began to weep as she watched her husband pile the blankets across her body once again.

"I'm always sick," she said, past tears. "I can't remember being well, anymore."

That was not true. She knew that she wept because she remembered the better times all too well. Once, it had seemed normal for her to feel beautiful. She well recalled playing games like *qallupiluq*, jumping from one high stone to another to avoid the boys—and how they had looked at her, standing fine and radiant above them. She remembered laughing down at their awestruck faces, feeling as though she had outshone the summer sun. Then the wind would catch at her long raven hair, bringing her locks to life as if they too wanted to tease the boys, and she would love the moment.

"Can't catch me," she muttered.

"What?" her husband asked, still smiling.

She loved that smile. It was what she had first noticed when she'd seen him, a guest in camp, paddling up to the rocky shore in his slim *qajaq*. It was as though he'd been created, that summer, just for her, born of the very sea. He had stayed, after that, travelling with the rest of the camp, and helping them catch autumn fish. And without the slightest awkwardness, as though he knew as well as she that he'd been authored for her alone, he had afterward requested her as his wife.

His only wife! He was hers, her greatest belonging, as surely a private treasure as the soapstone *qulliq* lamp which provided light for their home, and she had since entertained herself, here and there, with the thought that if he'd sought additional wives, she would refuse them. Yet it was, she knew, just a game of her own. She had always sensed, somehow, that theirs was a story of dual hearts—a single life that but pretended at separateness.

Or had she slipped into another dream?

"You'll be well," her husband whispered, his face now betraying concern. The sight of him, looking over her like that, seemed to awaken her from some febrile downturn, so that she half sat up in bed, crying out in alarm.

"How long have I been sick?" she demanded.

"Long," he answered, finding his smile again. His gentle voice, at once mellow and sure, seemed to meld like oil into her quivering sinews and shaken mind. She lay back, then, abandoning herself to his attentions.

"Sleep," he said, "and dream of how fine our children will be."

Children? Pilaaq almost laughed at the reference. With such a fever upon her, it would be some time before she could think of bearing children. She supposed that a mother's role was expected of her, though she had never developed an interest in children, as other camp girls had. It seemed possible that she wanted so much to *do*; to *see*; to live some of her life before giving it up toward childrearing. Besides, she'd seen what childbirth had done to some women. She was yet young and beautiful—a nascent bride. She wanted to thrive in the feel of that, maybe parade it before a few other girls, before someone bound her with the term of "mother."

It seemed, while her fever-dreams enwrapped her with such ideas, that she became almost sticky with the growing dread they engendered. She was dimly aware, at one half-conscious point or another, of batting her hands through the air, trying to tear away things like webs that fell in layers about her. First the tent, then the very hide blankets beneath and over her, came to feel like some immuring cocoon.

Pilaaq was next awakened by strange sounds. Though they were low, their pitch seemed to pierce her already aching head with a noise as of:

"Ti, ti, ti . . . "

Then another noise would come, just before the first few ended. This new noise was a more guttural sound, like a wet gurgle:

"Taaq . . . "

Pilaaq opened her eyes to see a dark object hovering near her lips, then a hint of vapour, and realized that it was a soup bowl.

Again, her husband was offering her broth.

She scowled, turning her head away from the bowl's edge.

Pilaaq's husband sighed, then straightened, pulling the bowl away until he held it with both hands in his lap. He knelt beside her, looking concerned.

"You hate me," she told him.

"Never," he said. "But you need to eat."

"Then find me something except that," she said, nodding toward the bowl. "I can't stand it."

"Your mother says seal broth is the best for a fever," he argued, smile looking strained.

"That's not seal," she said. "I can tell. It doesn't have any smell or taste. It's like hot phlegm . . . "

Again, Pilaaq's husband sighed. "You're just sick," he offered, as in times past. They had had this argument before, and he used every exact line, each time a new conflict arose. "You'll be able to smell and taste it—"

"Once I'm better," Pilaaq interrupted. "That's what you

keep saying. But I never get better."

After a moment, tears began to ooze from the edges of Pilaaq's eyes, and she added:

"I'm dying. I can feel it. I can feel my own life running away from me. Something's taking it from my veins."

Pilaaq's husband gave her a strange look, at once stern and sorrowful, placing a cool hand on her forehead. She could feel the sweat there, sliding between his palm and her brow.

"Don't be like that," he at last said. Then he smiled. He opened his mouth to say something further, but was interrupted by those strange noises Pilaaq had earlier heard. By now, some part of her had convinced itself that they'd been false sounds— another lurid production of her fever-dreams. Yet she heard them clearly, now, those dual and slightly overlapping noises of:

"Ti, ti, ti . . . "

"Taaq . . . "

"What's that?" she said, half-turning in bed. The noises had come from somewhere to the rear and right of her. Out of the corner of one eye, she could see a raised platform, perhaps as high as one's knee, piled with dark hides. On it, something moved.

The slight smile of Pilaaq's husband grew into a broad grin. "You're going to disturb our sons," he said.

Pilaaq was taken aback by the statement, and fell back fully on her pallet.

"What?" She was convinced that she had not heard her husband correctly.

"They're loud as they are strong, aren't they?" he asked, still grinning. He kept glancing back and forth between her and whatever she'd glimpsed.

"Who are?" Pilaaq demanded.

Her husband frowned, then, shifting his knees. "Our sons," he said. "Who else?"

"We don't have children," she told him, tone colder than a glacier's heart. She was almost certain that she hadn't slipped back into a fever dream. Was this really her husband speaking to her? Or was her true husband watching her even now, pitying her fitful frame, as it tossed unaware in the grip of nightmare?

Of a sudden, Pilaaq's husband looked ashen, his normally brazen face etched with concern. He made no answer for a long moment, then muttered:

"You're just sick . . . "

"No," she insisted, though her heart was now racing. "I'd know if I had children or not."

She would, wouldn't she? She had to.

Again, her husband went silent, dark eyes unblinking as they lay fixed upon her own. Then he turned his head, squeezing his eyes shut, and muttering:

"You're just sick . . . "

Pilaaq remembered screaming, then, cursing her husband as she fought her way upward from the sleeping pallet. Yet she was also weak, confused, and his unshakeable arms held her back down, until blackness arose to claim her awareness.

For the first time ever, she dreamt of butterflies.

She laughed under summer sun and chased butterflies, their wing-beats flashing black and yellow, through summer *paunnaq* flowers. The blossoms lay across every hill, like claret fire marching over dun slopes. And the butterflies grew ever more numerous as she chased, until they at last turned and she ran, giggling, from them. But they were no longer butterflies, by then, but admiring boys, and they called out that she was beautiful.

Pilaaq awoke at the strange sounds again. Still, she rolled to left and right, not immediately arising. She hated the feel of the sweat, like a small ocean, across every curve of flesh, and she used the blankets to wipe at her own body moisture, at last pushing the wet caribou hides down to twist in a pile at her feet.

"Ti, ti, ti . . . "

"Taaq . . . "

She rolled over, lying on her stomach to look up at the

raised platform behind her head. So, it had not been a fever dream. She could see the single bundle of swaddling robes, more caribou hide, and part of what it contained: tiny arms, hands moving, the roundness of partially haired heads. Babies.

Her sons?

Pilaaq was already shivering without the hides over her, the fever's grip tightening to remind her of its power. Yet she stared at the raised platform, at the bundle. Slowly, her limbs shaking and her jaw locked with the intensity of shivers, she brought herself to hands and knees. With even greater slowness, she began to creep toward the platform, one of her arms almost giving out beneath her. She made it, however, and soon knelt over the infants.

They seemed like twins, though it was impossible to tell for certain. And they did bear some resemblance to Pilaaq herself. Also, the more she stared, the more they seemed to resemble her husband. But could she simply be imagining such things? It still felt mad to think that, fevered as she'd been, she could not recall bearing children. When had she even been pregnant?

The boys, nestled beneath their mutual swaddling robes, seemed hardly to notice her. Their eyes were closed; and their constant, however torpid, movements reminded her of her own febrile tossing. Of a sudden, she felt a stick of concern in her breast—the most dim ember of protectiveness. Her children were not also ill, were they?

Tears welling in her eyes, as much from confusion as anxiety, she extended a single finger toward the infants. When it brushed the hand of one of them, the baby boy closed tiny fingers around her own. A line of water ran from one eye to her chin, and she whispered, "I don't remember you . . . "

There was the sound of flapping upon flapping, and Pilaaq's husband entered the tent. When he first saw Pilaaq out of bed, kneeling next to the twin boys, his eyes were wide with concern; but then they softened, and he smiled, urging Pilaaq back to her sleeping pallet.

As her husband was piling the caribou hides over her, Pilaaq whispered to him, "But I don't remember them. Don't say I'm just sick. I don't even remember carrying them."

"You were at the worst of your illness, then," her husband told her, his expression growing grave upon recounting such a thing. "It was a long time ago." He wiped at her forehead. "You barely survived," he added. "Nothing you said made any sense."

"I can't even remember their names," Pilaaq muttered.

"They don't have any," her husband said, suddenly beaming. "See? You recall some things. They're for you to name, when you wish. For now, I just call them our . . . Slippery Babies." He leaned back and gave a short laugh.

Of a sudden, Pilaaq was overwhelmed with weariness. She might have sped fast into sleep, had her insides not ridden an abrupt wave of nausea.

"Slippery Babies," she murmured, barely aware of anything but her husband's smile. "My Slippery Babies . . ."

"Sleep again," the warm voice of her husband told her. "And when you wake, there will be more broth for you."

Pilaaq wanted to protest, stimulated to sourness at the very idea of food, yet even speech was of a sudden too costly to her; too heavy a burden for her lips to manage. And the dreams, like dusty wings, arrived once again to enfold her.

As ever, fever savaged her mind, spinning its strands across her breath, until she lay bundled in silent scream. When the nightmares at last relented, as if they had grown tired of her wracked and broken selfhood, she came to stand upon dun slopes. There, paunnaq blossoms greeted her with purple fire, their dew giving drink to innumerable butterflies. She ran among them, teasing, until black and yellow rose to swirl about her, the gentle flutter of wings like kisses upon her cheeks.

Pilaaq awoke, once again, to the thin sounds of her sons:

"Ti, ti, ti . . ."

"Taaq . . ."

Still half in dream, she was overwhelmed by the sense of something clinging to her—and she thrust the caribou blankets with a snarl from her sweat-sheathed body. Almost immediately, she began to shiver, growing lucid; but she was glad of it.

"Ti, ti, ti . . . "

"Taaq . . . "

Pilaaq turned, regarding the moving forms on the raised platform behind her head. Those infants, it occurred to her, were noisier than ever. Perhaps they were hungry. Yet that presented a question to her: how had the infants, up till now, nursed? Pilaaq struggled to think clearly, wondering how many people might remain in camp, if any. Camp folk came and went, and Pilaaq had long been ill. It did not seem likely that her husband had managed to get the twins to nurse from her, sick as she was. Could it have been, then, that another woman had nursed them?

The thought kindled a possessive sort of outrage in Pilaaq's breast. Had another woman been providing for her children? That was not a strange idea; though Pilaaq, perhaps because she'd been denied any time—any memory—of her babies up till this point, found herself resenting the possibility.

It was only when Pilaaq tried to arise that she realized the degree to which weakness had housed itself in her once-splendid body. Scraping at whatever trace of strength yet remained in her, Pilaaq raised herself into a crawl, then approached the now-silent infants. Once, then twice, the inside of the tent seemed to grow dark, as though its lamp light had dimmed, but Pilaaq quickly understood that her own vision, her own consciousness, was at ebb. Still, she clamped her teeth together with each swoon, her abdomen hovering over the floor as if her elbows and knees were mere props; then, again, she forced herself to move.

When she at last knelt near the infants, nearly hovering over them, she was struck by the fact that their eyes were yet closed. It seemed strange that they were chubby and round in the face, moved like healthy babies, but they would not look at her.

Trying to reject the thought that they were ill, she wondered if they might be sleeping. She watched them for a long moment, her gaze following the gentle movements of their arms over the fur of the swaddling robes they shared. Their faces were serene, identical, as though each shared the other's dreams.

Eventually, with greatest care, Pilaaq moved her fingers toward one eyelid of the nearest twin. Fighting to still the trembling of her hands, for chills were upon her again, she touched the boy's eyelid, gently coaxing it open.

The iris was orange.

Pilaaq released the eyelid, stiffening in shock, so that her chills were forgotten.

Before she might form any opinion, the breath caught in her throat—for, of a sudden, both twins opened their eyes:

On the closest boy, the eyes were of an orange colouration, blazing with greater saturation than that of saffron lichen.

On the other boy, the eyes were luminous green.

Both of the twins, then, turned to meet Pilaaq's gaze, and their mouths opened to issue forth those lurid noises that had ever stolen her into wakefulness:

"Ti, ti, ti," trilled the twin with eyes of orange.

"Taaq," guggled the one whose orbs were green.

Pilaaq, at last finding her breath, released a rising whine of horror. What was she seeing? It was too crisp, too constant, for another fever dream. She had heard of sicknesses that turned the eyes white, even filled them with blood; but she had never heard of anything that invited such mad colouration.

After a moment, something unnameable arose from Pilaaq's centre—something sparking and wild that demanded she see the twins in their entirety. The impulse seemed to master her hand before she could counter it with rational thought, and she snatched outward, moving like the strike of a weasel, so that her hand grasped at the swaddling robes. Pilaaq tore them from the infants, casting the covering hides to the tent's floor.

The twin heads raised instant alarm at losing their swaddling robes—those same cries they had ever issued, but this time
their screams were louder and piercing to such a degree that Pilaaq was forced to cover her ears. At once, the cries were mingled
with her own scream, for the sounds, she saw, issued from one
source:

The twins were in fact a lone creature. When Pilaaq had
torn the swaddling robes away, she had not uncovered two baby
boys, but only a single being; a wormlike thing whose ends resembled infants. Where the chests of the twins would normally
have led to lower abdomens, then hips, then legs and feet, they
instead led into tubes bedecked in orange and green spots. The
voluptuous flesh came together at a common centre, a single body
that resembled nothing other than a caterpillar. Along that body,
Pilaaq could see other infantile hands, stubby and protruding like
larval legs, running along its pulsing length.

Then the tent shook, and there was that flapping upon
flapping near its mouth, that signalled the arrival of Pilaaq's husband.

What rushed into the tent was dressed like Pilaaq's husband, though its head was an obscene mass of insectile parts.
Bulbous eyes, occupying most of the head's mass, shimmered
like quartz in the lamp light—crowned with olive antennae like
colossal plumes. These antennae sought toward the wailing in-
fant-thing, while the head turned in inspection. The mockery of
Pilaaq's husband regarded the Slippery Babies for only a moment,
before turning back to Pilaaq herself.

Pilaaq, her throat choked with silent screams, watched
as a great tongue unrolled from under the husband-thing's head.
Tubular and of as luteous a colour as the first infant eye Pilaaq
had seen, the long organ curled and dangled for a moment. Then
it quivered, her husband's voice accompanying each vibration:

"I offered you motherhood. Family. If you had simply
slept for me. Simply dreamt for us."

Then the husband-thing snatched up the Slippery Babies in one arm. It turned back toward Pilaaq for one more moment, as though making a final decision. Then Pilaaq watched it tear at the tent, its fingers having grown together into attenuated, razor-like appendages.

The tent came apart across the ceiling, eventually falling open around Pilaaq. A great gust of wind caught up its edges, biting then numbing Pilaaq's skin, and she saw but the dark of winter around her. Wind-driven snow now lashed from every direction—and she knelt at the heart of murderous cold. She saw, and at last understood, that there had never been a camp, that she had never been other than a prisoner. The illusions eroded with speed about her, as though caught in the very wind, and she wondered if she had ever languished in a tent at all. It now seemed that the remnants of the structure around her, flapping like the tatters of some ruptured bladder, were more akin to a vast cocoon.

Wings unfurled, black and yellow, from the husband-thing's back, growing as if blown outward by the wind, until he stood before her as a great butterfly. Then the tortured air caught those wings and carried him upward. Like petals tossed to the storm, he was borne far into the darkness. Pilaaq could see him there, hovering within range of her vision for a single heartbeat's span, still bearing his Slippery Babies in arm. They—it—wailed, so that their voices merged with the wind.

Then all were gone.

Pilaaq lay in the surrounding darkness for some minutes, her eyes closed, feeling the cold devour, delving deep into her core, until it at last seemed warm as a friend's touch. She smiled when the honest sleep stole upon her, knowing that it would this time carry only dreams of paunnaq blossoms. Even now, she could feel the wind in her hair, as though it too wanted to tease the boys with her beauty. She laughed when they reached out to grasp her, finding nothing.

And she chased butterflies.

Ghost Flesh

It was deep in that moon time of *Saggarut*, when the caribou have shed their winter coats and grown the thinner fur of summer, that a starving man arrived upon a shore littered with shells.

The man was Saala, and he had fled his people wearing little more than the clothes of old caribou hide covering his weary skin. These were all he owned that were not stolen, and they were half of his total belongings. The other half of his holdings were comprised of the *qajaq*, the little one-man boat, that had brought him to this beach; as well as the double-ended paddle to make the boat move. He bore no bags with him, no tools or implements of the hunt—not even so much as a leather thong with which to tie back his raven locks. A chill summer wind swept hair like smoke over his face, as Saala dragged his stolen qajaq up onto the beach, and he wondered what he would eat.

Saala's eyes came to rest on the small heaps of purplish seaweed that had been cast up by the tides: all he might dine upon, for now, and perhaps for the rest of his potentially short life. His

139

sealskin boots rasped the tough shells together, underfoot, as he gave his paddle a kick, keeping it well away from the sea's grasp, before he began to gather his sole food source. Saala had not eaten for some time, and his browned hands trembled as he gathered the kelp.

Saala swallowed his last mouthful of seaweed minutes later, its blandness rendered tolerable between his need for salt and anything that might fill an empty gut. But it made Saala mindful only of real food. He turned in all directions, looking around at the cove where he had landed, feeling unnerved by the sight. High cliffs loomed in a semi-circle about him, as though some colossus had arisen from the sea in ages beyond memory, pressing a great thumb landward to stamp a beach out of dark rock. There were stones of various sizes in this place, however eldritch in shape and colour, as though they had once been massive seashells, standing higher than a man and having curves akin to those of a woman; and these were polished, smoothed so that their opalescent striations winkled in the sun, like pillars of ice half-melted at winter's end.

This was strange enough, but the *shells*.

Everywhere Saala's eyes travelled, far and near, there were seashells of all sizes and shapes: so many that they formed a barrier between boots and sand underneath; so many that the beach itself was made visible only where toes and heels stepped hard, burrowed deep. They shone like many tears in the golden light, grided underfoot with every step, and Saala wondered how long his boots would last in this place.

Inland, he thought, *for drinking water. Or keep paddling, find better beach.*

He didn't like this beach.

But he was so weary, and even the most essential concerns seemed to wander far from the reaches of his awareness, like a paddle left too close to the greedy tide. The sun soaked like warm oil into Saala's flesh, and the lap of waters was as a mother's gentle song. There came a moment when Saala realized that he was sitting—his back to one of the woman-shaped rocks, remnants of his salty meal yet clutched in hand—though he neither remembered approaching the strange stones, nor recalled sitting down. He was tired, though, and numb beyond sadness, so questions were like unwelcome guests within his mind.

Saala's sleep was uneasy, as in a fever, his senses of wakefulness and dream admixed like swirling oils across water. He might have cried out several times, or dreamed such, though he was certain of awakening only once, and briefly. It was a thought that seemed to awaken him, dire and flushed with urgency:

Where are the birds?

The cliffs around him should have echoed with their screeches and piping. The sky overhead should have been streaked with their careening silhouettes.

And the mosquitoes? he wondered. In this month, a cloud of them should have been on him with every ebb of the wind.

The flies? When had there been anything that flew or hopped or crawled, even when Saala had gathered seaweed to eat?

But the panic that had awakened Saala was already gone, and with it whatever had sustained such thoughts, so that they receded as quickly as they had arisen, like collops of meat stirred about in soup. Saala's mind soon embraced the more usual offerings of dream: blinding gold across seawater; lichen-covered stones of beloved gravesites; the voices of people he knew, threatening to shoot him with arrows.

Saala awakened in shadow.

He immediately realized that he had slept overlong, since the sun had swung round to the other side of the sky. In this season, it would not set, but would only make circles about the heavens, before it at last fell to leave another lightless half-year. Saala had heard of the sun behaving differently in other lands, and especially as one moved far inland, though he was little travelled until now; and this was the only sun he had ever known. Now, the radiant disk had hidden itself on the landward side of the cliffs, so that the cliff walls were black as winter, the highest and lowest points of them perfectly outlined against the glow beyond. The beach lay in shadow, seashells showing like a field of ancient bones.

Saala was startled when he realized that he was not hearing wind and surf alone, but the sounds of voice. It was a strange voice, neither male nor female at first, and it rose in strength only as Saala's attention became fixed on it. As Saala listened, the words seemed to evolve from a sort of low babble to a rhythmic drone, then to an actual song:

> *Gladly, I crawled from my mother's belly,*
> *And sun seemed to ignite my limbs from within,*
> *As if the strength she had given me,*
> *Were finest oil lit on emergence.*
> *In this way am I the lamp of my parents' light,*
> *Illuming the way of generations.*
>
> *Holy, I bathed in my father's breath,*
> *And stars seemed to clothe me like amulets,*
> *As if the kiss of his blessings,*
> *Had seated me upon mountains.*
> *Here am I carved bowl, my parents' to fill,*
> *Brought even to lips of parents unborn.*
>
> *Embrace me, worlds unimagined!*
> *I am of these owned; nothing other:*
> *Giving what you seek in me;*
> *Taking what asked to take.*
> *Let this flame guide you from direst places,*
> *Before it tricks you toward the same.*

Saala was of a sudden very thirsty, and the base lust for water drove his mind to full wakefulness. Still, the song repeated itself—no dream. It was a man's voice in gentle tune, as though in singing to a child, and Saala realized that he was not alone on this beach. Yet who was there in sight?

As Saala gazed around, eventually toward the water, he came to a realization so horrifying that it nearly eclipsed his wonder at the mysterious song: the tide had come in. The water, many paces away when Saala had fallen asleep, had crept nearly as far as Saala himself, and now lapped only an arm's length from the tips of his boots.

Saala nearly leapt into a crouch, the stiffness of sleep making him teeter, reach out a hand for balance as shells ground together beneath him. His sleep-fogged eyes made their way from one end of the beach to the other, and his heart beat ever faster within him. Terror seemed to well in some spot beneath his throat.

Nowhere in sight, he thought.

Saala stood, eyes sweeping the beach yet again.

They were gone. Paddle and qajaq were gone.

"Huqutaunngittutuk!" Saala swore—an ancient curse and a futile one. By falling asleep without keeping his belongings far from the tide, he had as good as killed himself. Circumstances had been bad enough, since the flight from his people, with no tools or food or drinking water. But now he had no transportation. Going overland in this season was sure to starve him, even assuming he could defeat the cliff heights without breaking his neck. His panic was such that reason failed, for a moment, and the idea of swimming, like a walrus or bear, flashed through his mind for a half-second. The idea died as it was replaced by the image of himself, bobbing, blue, dead of cold before managing even minutes amongst the summer waves.

What was there to do now?

But then Saala became mindful of the song, which had dwindled in volume but not altogether ceased, and his mind seized upon the mysterious voice with renewed interest.

Peering around the nacreous pillar of rock against which

he'd slept, Saala's eyes searched the shadowed beach, but found no singer. He went, then, among the other stones, so alike to the curves of swaying women, and Saala could not quite find the courage to call out. He did not wish to alarm whomever was singing. It sounded like an old man, though Saala would have welcomed anyone at this point. He had originally wanted to avoid Human contact, when he'd first stolen the qajaq and fled, but there was now no choice in re-embracing Humanity. The singer had to have come from some camp or other, a place full of tools and food and water and life; Saala was now without any but the latter, and life was sure to forsake him soon.

Saala's mouth was open as he rounded the last standing rock, preparing to call out, but the greeting died in his throat. He was aware, first, of a strange light, a glow as of some moon that had descended to rest upon the shells of the beach. But Saala was aware, within a moment of his stepping toward it, that the silver aura in fact surrounded—in fact, *was*—a single man. And Saala froze, then, eyes wide to regard this man, the singer of the arcane little song. It was a man of middle age, perhaps older, though years were difficult to tell, since every detail of his flesh, hair, and clothes (not dissimilar to Saala's own) were of that uniform moonlight hue. That silvern light seemed to make up the very substance of the man, so that he knelt upon the shells of the beach like some great, moon-carven lamp.

Saala might have stood for minutes, listening to the repeated drone of the moon-man's song, though the figure never seemed to notice Saala even in those rare times when he looked up, revealing distant, slightly amused eyes. Mostly, the argentine features sang down to hands of equal hue, to fingers positioned as though they held tiny objects that only the singer could see.

A *pajaq*, Saala guessed—a visitant; the vision of one past or soon to be dead. Or was this something more sinister, something whose attention it would be best to avoid? Was this some manifestation of an *Ijiraq*, one of the Hidden Ones?

With thumb and forefinger, Saala rubbed at the area between his eyes, backing away.

Somewhere high up on the cliffs, to Saala's flank, there was the abrupt sound of a dull snap, or of something like an old hide flapped once in the wind. Saala did not see the origin of the sound, his eyes were so fixed on the moonlit singer, but his peripheral vision caught something—a blur of white and blue—as it hit a standing stone next to him. The object struck with fury, with a sound as of glacial ice hurled down from the heights. Saala sprang from the small explosion, nervous reflex jerking at him like strings, though flecks of cold yet managed to sting his cheek.

Saala whirled in a half-crouch, tight, breath suspended, as though he were some lemming in a bird's shadow. He rubbed at his cheek, staring at the place where the unknown missile had struck rock.

It was an arrow.

The first feature Saala noted was the fletching, which was bluer than a glacier's veins. It lined a shaft the colour of new-fallen snow, and this seemed to steam like breath or hot blood in the summer air. The arrow sat at an angle, seething like a thing alive, stuck at about face level in the woman-shaped pillar of rock. Saala's eyes followed the shaft's angle up toward the cliffs, but he could see no archer. His eyes were drawn back to the arrow as it loosed a strange hiss, then dissolved like an icicle under a flood of boiling water. It left no trace of moisture, however, nor any other sign that it had been there, other than a perfect hole in the rock.

Here was Strength, Saala knew, and his teeth were clenched with fear.

"What are you that you know the dead?" called a voice from the cliffs. Was the sound that of a woman? It seemed to ring all around, but Saala could see nothing of its owner.

Saala made no answer, but backed away from the dark edifice, until he felt another standing stone at his back. With hands upon the cool rock, but eyes on the heights, he guided himself still backward, around the stone, taking shelter behind its curves.

"The eggs are boiled," said a voice behind him.

Saala wheeled, terrified, and saw yet another silvern figure. This time, it was an elderly woman in finely made clothes, the stripes of their white fur edging showing despite the overall glow of her form. Like the singing man, this visitant was not looking at Saala. She passed by him, smiling, but with faraway eyes as she muttered:

"The eggs are boiled. Come eat . . . "

Saala was now aware of other noises as the beach came alive. His eyes wide and unblinking, he found silver-lit figures everywhere he turned. Men and women, most quite old, and all aglow, sat or rocked or walked from one end of the beach to another, so that the shells beneath them spangled, quartz-like, in the light of their bodies. Many spoke, mumbling incoherently, while others sang like the first figure Saala had seen. It was as though, in looking for them, Saala's very regard drew them from the shells of the beach. The shock of their numbers at last forced Saala's eyes to shut, as though they were some strange dream he might have dismissed through denial.

Another explosion—a new arrow, Saala now knew—shocked his eyes into opening. Somehow, he had failed to entirely shelter himself behind the standing stones, and the archer on the cliffs had found a new angle from which to attack him. Saala cringed, staring at the latest arrow, which was already hissing as it melted away from the rock in which it had stuck.

"Please!" Saala cried out, his voice echoing a bit and making him feel small as it met the cliff-sides. "I'm trapped here! Help me to go, and I'll go!"

Saala stood, still shaking, his chest feeling tight and sunken as he envisioned an arrow finding it. The mutterings of the moon-people surrounded him.

Saala's eyes then espied a form, pale against the shadows of the cliffs, and high above him. There was no hope, as Saala watched, that it was a Human being—since the figure leapt from one part of the cliffs to another, almost as though in short, arcuate flights. The agility—the sheer power of the leaps—was beyond all Human capacity, and Saala was again forced to wonder what kind of being his eyes beheld. He watched, though, knowing that the figure might put an arrow in him at any time it so desired, so there was no point in backing away.

Leaping left, leaping right; zigzagging downward in this way, the pale form descended toward the beach.

When the being stood almost upon the beach, still on cliff-stone, but within an arm's reach of the shells beneath it, the stranger paused. The first features of the being that Saala could be sure of included the bow held in hand—as well as the hand itself. Faint light seemed to emanate from both. The spangle of the bow was subtle, shifting, and multi-hued, reminding Saala of striated quartz washed under a sun-bathed stream. In fleeting moments, it reminded Saala of lamp-light viewed through a piece of ice. The hand that gripped it was clothed in a mitt, azure of hue, glowing so that it emphasized strange patterns across its surface.

The being, all white in either clothes or flesh (Saala could not tell), blinked twice. It blinked with eyes that were like blue moons, azure rings about great black pupils; and, but for their colour, they made Saala think of only one animal: an owl.

The strange being blinked a third time, otherwise poised in the perfect stillness of its crouch. Then, like a feather set adrift in gentle wind, it leapt from its shadowed perch, alighting with a crunch on the shells of the beach. Saala's attention was divided between those luminous eyes and the bow, held far from the being's body; and he could now see that the weapon dripped something like slush—globs of hissing ice that disappeared before touching the ground.

In a half-stalk, eyes now unblinking, the being neared Saala with great slowness, as though either expecting an attack or readying for the need to attack. Like one of the standing stones around him, Saala remained rigid and near breathless, watching the being's approach. Moonlit visitants mumbled, cackled and crooned, sometimes passing between Saala and the bow-wielder, as though unaware of either.

Not clothing, Saala thought. *Feathers.*

So, his guess at the eyes had been a good one. As the bow-wielder came to within a dozen paces of Saala, he could see that, other than the strange mitt, it was without clothing—bearing only feathers whiter than snow. The being was an admixture of Human and owl, having four limbs sharing in the lush plumage of the body, though the arms were somewhat alar in appearance, feathers trailing like exaggerated tassels from shoulders to hands. In the hand opposite the mitt, those feathers came over whatever the being used for fingers, so that staring at the limb was like beholding something as easily called "wing" as "arm."

A single word rose to set itself in Saala's mind: *Ukpiaapik*. Saala, like anyone who had heard the mutterings of elders, had collected some memories of the Animal Folk—of the varying forms they liked to adopt. But Saala had never imagined what shape those of the owl set might take.

The owl-being's nearness also gave Saala another chance to appreciate mitt and bow. He saw, now, that the mitt was strangely wrought, as though it were a two-fingered glove, with index and middle fingers meant to rest in one part, ring and pinky fingers in the other. Saala could further see that the markings on the mitt were Strong, squirming about like kicking sea-lice, as though the markings sensed Saala's scrutiny and refused to be viewed as a static pattern.

No string, Saala thought.

It was strange that that bow, so akin to sparks illuming ice from within, was not strung. Saala wondered if the Ukpiaapik had unstrung it before ascending to the beach.

Saala's curiosity was answered as the owl-being paused, raising the bow as though to sight in upon Saala. Then the bow

dipped, and the Ukpiaapik's opposite hand seemed to strum at the space within the curve of the weapon, as though stroking at unseen sinew. The bow's response was immediate, and an icy arrow streaked from the thing, finding a home near Saala's feet. Saala raised his arms against a spray of ice and minute shells—sent up like tiny sling-stones—to bite at hands and face.

The bow was a thing of Strength, and spawned its own arrows.

"Please!" Saala cried. He held up his hands to show that he had no weapons of his own.

"Turn back to me," came the owl-being's voice. It was smooth, having the faintest pipe to it, as though it were a small voice whistling within a larger one. To Saala, it sounded womanly.

"Show me your face again," the woman-owl demanded. "Or I'll examine it on your corpse."

The face issuing the demands to see Saala's own was almost wholly that of an owl, except that its eyes were blue, the same colour as the mitt holding the bow. The eyes seemed to glare at Saala from over a small ebon beak, barely moving as the being spoke. Beneath the beak, around what might have been a neck, there dangled talismans carven to resemble expressionless Human faces, these spangling in faint azure and silver, as though their spirits rested somewhere between wearer and visitants of the beach.

"Your face," the Ukpiaapik pressed. "I'll ask once more."

Saala turned to face the woman-owl, who stood for a moment, staring, before she released a small whistle.

"You bear the *kigjugaq*," she said.

With thumb and forefinger, Saala rubbed at the area between his eyes. It was usually an unconscious gesture—now a self-conscious one.

"If you tattooed it there yourself," the Ukpiaapik said, "after murdering some man or woman, it will not protect you."

Saala said nothing.

"But," the woman-owl added, "if it came to you because

you killed an Ijiraq, there is no shame in it. So, tell now, why do you hide it from me?"

Saala did not wish to answer. He did not wish to be there; but neither did he wish to feel one of those algid arrows sampling his heart. He had always heard that the Animal Folk, of which this owl creature seemed to be, were temperamental but reasonable. A few, however—especially those who had lived too long apart from their kind, and in the stranger parts of the Land—could go strange in the head.

What could she want from him? He had left his people because he'd wanted to be alone.

Should have known, Saala thought to himself.

The tattoo between his eyes would forever mark him as something to be feared; to be branded apart; to be thought of as less than Human.

"If," the Ukpiaapik said, "you are a murderer—"

"I'm no murderer," Saala said, cutting her off. His voice arose from anger, despite his fear. "Though I'll kill," he added, "to protect my *self*."

The woman-owl seemed startled by the outburst, but nodded at the words. "Of course," she said, "to protect yourself, but—"

"No," Saala interrupted. "Not to protect myself. To protect my *self*."

The Ukpiaapik blinked three times, perhaps taken aback. But she had lowered her bow. She yet held it far from her body, clenching the Strong weapon in that peculiar split mitt of hers, as if it were a thing that might have bitten even its wielder; but at least it was no longer inclined toward Saala.

Saala sighed with the weight of this encounter. There he was, like some mollusc relying upon a wearying shell, whilst curious birds pecked at him from above. And he realized, in that moment, that the guardian of this beach would settle for nothing less than his story.

He would tell her, then, but just enough. He would tell
her of that which had seared a kigjugaq beneath his brow, and of
that which he sought to escape. And he would let her guess at the
rest—the rest of his self. If she could not . . .

"I stink of graves," Saala told her. He pointed to the spot
between his eyes, the spot he so hated. "I've stunk of them since
the day of this. Since the Strength of the Land burned it into me."

The woman-owl nodded. She hunkered down, in the aspect of a listener. Without thinking, it seemed, she let the lowest
tip of her weapon touch shells of the beach: instantly, ice spread
outward from the site—a racing frost that crackled its way like
white flame across the piled seashells. Before the hungry rime
touched her plumed feet, however, the Ukpiaapik noticed, lifting
the bow again into open air, so that the freezing patch ceased to
burgeon. She seemed to think nothing of the incident, as though
she were used to accidents around such an implement of awful
Strength. Her great blue eyes re-fixed upon Saala's own.

After a moment of silence, Saala turned his back to the
woman-owl, viewing the many silvern figures who wandered and
gesticulated across the beach. He stared out past the sprawling
shadows of the cliffs, and almost smiled to see the sunlit flash of
waves, as though a thousand golden fish had arisen, wriggling,
out there on the sea. He spoke to those waves, and not to the
Ukpiaapik; and that made the story easier:

"It was the last time," Saala said, "I ever hunted. That's
when the Ijiraq came. I was on the Land with my hunting partner,
Sivuliq. Sivuliq and I . . . we hunted in a place too long. My grandmother told me about such places. Said we should never stand
too long in the *miqquugaq*—the places where plants grow bushy.
With the Strength that sets there."

Saala glanced back at the woman-owl, who did not inter-
rupt. But she nodded at his last few words, and Saala nodded
along with her, knowing that she had anticipated what he would
next say:

"These are the places the Hidden Ones like," he went on. "When the Ijiraq came, there was no warning. I heard a sound, but it was from my partner, Sivuliq. It sounded like he . . . like he had a bone in his throat. I turned. The Ijiraq was already on him. In him. A giant. Like many skins of fishes that had been piled. Rotted. Its head was fleshless and like the skull of a dog. Its hands were like split stones. Like blades of flint."

Saala found himself staring at his own hands, the fingers of which were curling as though to make claws. He lowered them, saying:

"It had opened up Sivuliq. It held him as though it wanted to step into his insides. And Sivuliq was . . . he was alive. He looked at me. Shook. But he didn't make a noise. It was like the Ijiraq had stolen his screams. The Ijiraq . . . it seemed . . . I don't know. It dipped near him, almost inside, where its hands were. It seemed to sniff something up out of Sivuliq. Something coloured like fish-bellies. Its mouth moved. Like a man eating. That's how it was. It was eating Sivuliq. But not his flesh. It was like it found a . . . secret meat inside him. Like there were two of my partner, one inside the other. And the other, the unseen, it was being sucked up."

Again, Saala glanced at the Ukpiaapik. She was looking to left and right, at the silvern visitants wandering the beach, as though Saala's words had somehow made her mindful of them. She noticed him watching her, and again settled azure eyes upon him, waiting. Saala turned from her, trying to find renewed comfort in the play of the waves, and failing, before he said:

"The Ijiraq didn't want me to see what it was doing to Sivuliq. It put its back to me, till it was finished. Then it dropped my partner. Dead. I had failed Sivuliq. Failed his family, who blamed me after. That was right, because I was wrong. I was afraid. Afraid of the Strength of that Hidden One."

"The Hidden Ones are as Strong as the Animal Folk," the woman-owl called to his back. "Their cunning is as great as our discipline. Their bale is as great as our grace. What could you have done?"

"Not what," Saala said, turning to regard her. "When. I knew a Strong *irinaliut*. Very Strong. The words of it have been passed through my grandmother's family since anyone can remember. She taught it to me when I began to hunt. Made me memorize it. Said it could strike, even kill, something as Strong as a Hidden One. We're Strong, my family."

The Ukpiaapik hissed, understanding. Her eyes were unblinking.

"I could have struck the Ijiraq," Saala continued, "when I saw it. I don't know if I could have saved my partner. I could have tried. For certain. But when I saw . . . what it was doing . . . I could not move."

"Terror is common to most beings," the woman-owl said.

Saala stared at her, shocked at her words. He almost laughed.

"But I did use my grandmother's irinaliut," Saala eventually went on. He was of a sudden weary, as though his listener's lack of understanding had become a new weight upon him. "I struck the Ijiraq with Strength," he murmured. He waved a grimy, calloused hand. "And I watched its own Strength pour out of it. Like water. From . . . a torn bladder."

"Then came pain," the Ukpiaapik said.

"Then came pain," Saala said, barely hearing her. "Like someone had rubbed embers between my eyes. I turned circles with it. Round. Round. Like a crazy dog."

And Saala half-turned, as though memory alone had jigged at his body like some invisible fish-line.

"I rubbed snow into it," Saala said. "It didn't help. But that pain went on the way home." He paused, thinking. "That was before the real pain. It was before people saw me. Told me what sat between my eyes. 'What's wrong with him?' children said. 'What's right?' I wanted to say back. The adults said a lot of nothing. But . . . the eyes! I never knew you could be *looked* at like that. It was like they'd never known me before. Only a couple of elders spoke to me. To say what the kigjugaq meant. To say I'd wear it forever."

"But it is a mark of pride," the woman-owl said. "It means you are Strong, that you have a destiny in killing the abominations of the Land."

Laughter, like a thing escaping some barrier, poured from between Saala's teeth. When it at last ebbed, Saala was able to answer:

"Then the proud are shunned. The destined live with the dead. Snow, ice, they melted. Summer came. Still, no one spoke to me. Not even the elders, after a while. They would just *look*. Between my eyes. Sivuliq's family moved away from camp almost right away. They acted like I killed my partner. I didn't blame them. That left only a couple of families besides my own. People, they never say anything. Always just *look*. When they moved, I moved, too. I stayed with them. What else to do? Until I began to hear what the children were saying. They're never careful, those. They would play with each other, sing strange songs:

Play, picking bird eggs;
Picking two, getting three.
Is there someone we forgot?
The boy who stayed too long,
Thought he was eating eggs;
He just ate the dead.

"It was something like that. But I could tell they were singing about me. And I knew where they got those ideas. Children always listen to grownups talking. Grownups just forget how they used to do it, too. So I knew people thought I was changed. Something of bad Strength. Like the Ijiraq."

Saala sighed. A long moment passed, wherein he watched

a luminous old woman rock herself, pointing, laughing at something unseen, before he continued:

"And that's what drove me to the graves. There were graves overland. A few. Not far from camp. Piled rocks over old bones. And they were quiet. Simple. I felt like . . . they pulled me to that place. Like they were the opposite of camp. Understanding. Simple. Not always . . . *looking*. Not all the bones were in the graves. They were white and beautiful. Some with lichen on them. And I liked to . . . touch them sometimes. Just put a finger on them. And I never gave the whistle—the one you're supposed to. To protect yourself from death, when you touch a bone? And they never hurt me. It's like they . . . knew me. Knew I wanted to keep them company. Knew who I was."

"They knew," the Ukpiaapik echoed.

"I built a little sod house there," Saala went on. "After a while. But it was no good. It was like the dead stopped speaking to me. Stopped feeling like they recognized me. Even became afraid of me, like my own family. After a while. And people would come . . . *look* at me. Sometimes. *Look* at me like the childrens' song was right. I knew, then. I knew I had to get away. I had to go where no one would look. I almost didn't manage to do it. It was hard to get brave enough. But I knew the camp would move away soon. It would move, and winter would come, and I'd have no chance. So I went to camp one last time. When most people were asleep. I . . . stole a qajaq. And a paddle."

"And thus you arrived to this place," the woman-owl said.

Saala chuckled, but it was without true humour. "Almost not," he said. "Children saw me. Ran to parents, because I was a monster. My own cousins shot arrows at me. Like you."

"It was a warning," the Ukpiaapik piped, her tone laced with what might have been pity. "I did not know whether to call you man or Ijiraq. I watched you from the heights, saw you sleep while your qajaq and paddle were devoured by creeping tide."

Tears, leaking past the numbness to which Saala had become accustomed, made the woman-owl seem like a pale blur. "Why?" Saala asked like a child. "Why didn't you wake me?"

"If I had been sure of that which I am now," the Ukpiaapik said, standing and approaching Saala until she was within arm's reach, "I would not have done so for all of the Land's bounty."

She blinked thrice, her eyes like sky-coloured lamps.

"I am the protector of this place," she told him. Saala watched as the woman-owl turned round, light as a dancer, careful not let her deadly bow come too close to him. "You have arrived upon a sacred shore," the Ukpiaapik went on, "and by a turn of destiny alone. For is it not clear? You are the helper I have wept and prayed for, come at last."

Saala stood unspeaking, uncomprehending, while the light babble of visitants rose and fell around him.

"That silver-lit folk you see and hear," the woman-owl told him, "are not true visitants, for not even the Strongest can capture the true soul, much less bind it to the Land. But there is nevertheless a kind of Strength in living fibre—a ghost flesh, invisible and quick, which brings vibrancy to the more vulgar meat and mind. You see it preserved in this place. It walks, discourses with itself, and in most ways resembles those individuals—now passed into mystery—who once bore it."

Saala could feel his breath quickening at the idea. "But . . . what does this mean?" he asked.

The Ukpiaapik shrugged. "Can you really have no idea?" she asked in turn. "There are powers in the Land. Agonies. And these, of old, have understood that the experiences of generations must be preserved. Yes, the Humankind pass down their knowledge from one brood to the next, but such is always via the spoken word. What calamity, then, when the teachers perish before their word may be passed! There are disasters: harsh winters, diseases, hazards of the Land such as what you have already endured. The way of the Humankind, with the old commingling to give rise to the young, is at once the greatest of strengths and weaknesses.

Culture, tradition: these are too brittle to trust in the hands of living generations. Knowledge, wisdom: these are too fragile to weather the aeons. How else, then, to preserve it?"

The woman-owl gestured around herself, toward the figures across the beach; and Saala frowned, guessing at what she meant. Was she trying to say that these visitants—no, not visitants—were somehow like copies of once-living folk? Saala nodded, beginning to understand: these were great people, old people, those whose knowledge was worth preserving. Saala was neither looking at body or spirit, in this folk, but something akin to footprints in clay. Shells long shed and enduring past the lives that had borne them. He was looking at something carnal, yet deeper, even, than supporting bones.

"Ghost flesh?" Saala murmured, eyes flashing across the beach.

"Ghost flesh," the Ukpiaapik said, "if one wishes to call it such. If there were any other man here, he might feel a chill, imagine that he had heard or brushed up against something unseemly. But you—you bear *that* between your eyes."

Saala's eyes were elsewhere, though he knew that the woman-owl was now pointing toward his head.

"And the kigjugaq," she said, "marks you as one who has grown closer to the substance of an Ijiraq, by testing your Strength against its own. You now know the Hidden portion of the world, for your eyes have to some extent been claimed by it. Thus can you see the ghost flesh in which those around you walk. It is . . . what the Ijiraq sought when it attacked your partner. Something that we have herein removed and preserved by means of Strength."

Saala nodded. "And you guard it?" he asked.

"It must be guarded," the Ukpiaapik explained. "The stuff you choose to call ghost flesh may live forever, if untouched. But the Hidden Ones and their ilk relish it, and would devour every figure aglow upon this beach, were I to let them. Their hunger would see the ghost flesh as ardency's essence. When taken in, the flesh is as a burning brand, whether glorious or destructive, consumed. It makes an Ijiraq mad with pleasure—not of the sort one would feel with love, or even upon eating delicious food, but as upon seeing a spark in darkness, or filling a barren hollow with the memory of life. My guardianship, then, has meant constant siege, and I have lost count of how many winters and summers have passed, in which the Hidden Ones have arisen from the waves, snatching at those I protect. But know that I have never failed, and many Hidden Ones—and things more bale than they—have fallen before those weapons given to my trust."

Upon these last words, the woman-owl brandished her bow, yet dripping with its frost of arcane Strength.

"How has fate brought me here?" Saala murmured. A chill wind arose; but it was some small pleasure to Saala, so that he closed his eyes, letting it dry the tears upon his burning cheeks.

Then a remarkable thing occurred: Saala heard the graunch of seashells underfoot, as the Ukpiaapik approached, and his eyes opened just as she took his hand in that hand of hers which did not bear the strange mitt, and he found that she did indeed possess fingers—warm and fine beneath soft plumes.

"But I have guarded this place alone," the woman-owl told him.

Saala did not answer, but neither did he pull away. He regarded her face for a time, as it was now near to his own, and he noted how there were other features admixed with those of an owl. It was a bird's face—yes—but it was also a woman's.

They walked together, after that, the sea's wind cooling both of them, and the vast shadow of the cliff retreated a bit as the sun shifted round. They roamed over piles of shells, around nacreous stones with the curves of dancing women, and the Ukpiaapik spoke, whispering to Saala something of the beach's secrets. She spoke of Hidden paths and fortifications carven by means of Strength, none of which might be espied from the beach itself. She spoke of the strangest or most comical of the beach's ghost flesh inhabitants. She sang, for Saala, a few of the songs with which she entertained them on moonless nights; sang in a secret tongue she promised to teach him at a later time. She told Saala of the Strength that would sustain life and heal wounds whilst he joined her in guardianship of this place. She spoke of the rich foods, shellfish and kelp, that pacts with the sea powers provided. She spoke, also, of her fierce and lonely battles with the devourers who arose from the waves—foes that were mostly Hidden Ones, but at other times horrors conceived in the womb of lightless deep.

Most importantly, she whispered to Saala the secret of the seashells, of how the bulk of the shells hid greater shells, eternal and deep, to which the beings of ghost flesh were tied. These, she explained, were homes to the ghost-fleshed, who squeezed themselves inside like numinous crabs. They slept whenever their strange whimsies did not drive them to walk the beach.

"And with you come at last," the woman-owl at last told him, "it is no longer I who will bear this knowledge alone." She stood, as she spoke, the sea's waters lapping at the plumes about her ankles, as though the ocean's cold meant nothing to her. Her eyes were turned toward the gold of the waves, as though to thank the qajaq and paddle that had floated away upon a sleeping Saala, her aspect no longer martial.

"No," Saala agreed. He dared not step so far into the water, though he stood close behind her, his sealskin boots awash with tidal foam.

That was when he pushed.

A great push was required, with both hands: Saala barely managed to put his full strength into it, before he was forced to leap backward, away from the surf.

When Saala's outstretched hands drove between her shoulder-blades, the Ukpiaapik loosed a high, piping cry, as she fell forward into deeper water.

The effect was immediate:

The lower half of the spangling bow dipped into the sea-water, and there remained—for a white half-sphere of ice exploded outward from around where it had touched the ocean. Like a gelid shockwave, the ice caught the woman-owl, freezing her into a still-spreading circle of hoar. Part of her body remained above the ice, suspended like that, along with the upper portion of her head, perhaps somewhere around her eyes.

Saala stepped even further backward as the ice crept up onto some of the beach's shells. For a long moment, he stood staring, worrying that the ice might never cease to creep outward from the bow. But the sea, in time, seemed to win back something of itself, as though the Strength in that marvellous weapon had drained like blood into its vastness; so that which was left in the water was akin to a peculiar iceberg, bobbing with the rigid Ukpi-aapik near its centre. Saala regarded her half-submerged form for some time, looking for signs of movement, but there were none, and he grunted in satisfaction, guessing that whatever she used for flesh and bone had frozen as surely as the water itself.

Saala sang, then, for a time; for, while he was tired and hungry, there was no longer any hurry for anything. He might have sung to the dead woman-owl. He might have sung to those people of ghost flesh, uncomprehending and incomprehensible, muttering at his back. He might even have sung to the Ijiraq, long gone, who had altered his essence to that of the *Ione*. Did the dedication matter? Even his song was a theft:

Gladly, I crawled from my mother's belly,
And sun seemed to ignite my limbs from within,
As if the strength she had given me,
Were finest oil lit on emergence.
In this way am I the lamp of my parents' light,
Illuming the way of generations.

Holy, I bathed in my father's breath,
And stars seemed to clothe me like amulets,
As if the kiss of his blessings,
Had seated me upon mountains.
Here am I carved bowl, my parents' to fill,
Brought even to lips of parents unborn.

Embrace me, worlds unimagined!
I am of these owned; nothing other:
Giving what you seek in me;
Taking what asked to take.
Let this flame guide you from direst places,
Before it tricks you toward the same.

Saala grew tired of singing, the hunger rising in him until even the chill sea-wind could not cool his burning face. He turned, then, away from the sea. He turned to eye the nearest of those who roamed in ghost flesh, imagining the fervour, the fire, they might lend him—if only for the most blessed shards of time. And under them, he now knew, were those ghost-fleshed who yet slumbered in their seashell homes. It would take some time, perhaps, to find those shells, to learn how the ghost flesh might be pried out of them. But was fine food not worthy of great endeavour?

Now, Saala failed to see anything in the darkness of his self, which he had vowed to ever fight for, other than those embers of hunger to which the Ukpiaapik had drawn his awareness. He was as his qajaq and paddle—snatched away upon stranger tides, whilst the living had slept. The Humankind, so obsessed with their traditions, with their preservation of knowledge, might once have embraced him. How might he now embrace anything of them in return? With such thoughts, Saala rubbed at the kigjugaq mark between his eyes: the one memento of his only true teacher, the Ijiraq, who had taught him the only lesson worth remembering.

Moving up the beach, Saala began to feast.

Drum's Sound

On the day when Kavinnguaq's camp last saw the sun, Kavinnguaq himself was presented with his first amulet. This was
in the moon time of *Akullit*, that of the warm and quite short
"middle season;" when the caribou are free of warble-flies, and it
is time to gather their hides for the approaching winter.

It was an unusual sort of amulet, carved from a wodge of
walrus tusk. It was fine, small enough to easily hide Kavinnguaq's
palm—which was in itself small, since Kavinnguaq was not then
old enough to have accompanied any adult on a hunting expedi-
tion.

Not that Kavinnguaq had ever expected to know such an
outing. He did not have normal parents, as other boys did. His
parents were already wizened, old enough that not a single black
hair stood upon their silvered heads. His father was the oldest of
the pair, and his hunting years were far behind him.

Still, Kavinnguaq was a healthy boy, a stranger to starvation, since his parents had never lacked for food. Each was an *Angakkuq*, and while Kavinnguaq had never pretended to understand the term (or the others his mother and father bandied about), he had at least gathered that his parents were specialists in those aspects of the world they at times called "Some Seen." The fact of being an Angakkuq further seemed to have something to do with the peculiar demands his parents made of Kavinnguaq himself, even other folk, from time to time: there was meat, for example, certain parts of which Kavinnguaq was not allowed to eat. There was fire and water, substances he was allowed to handle only at certain times. He had to watch where he blew the merest puff of breath. He also had to breathe in different ways, depending on where he stood out among the hills. He was made to wash his hands after certain happenings—or forbidden to do so, after different happenings. His parents seemed unperturbed by many of the behaviours other parents considered atrocious in children, while Kavinnguaq's minor transgressions shook them for no apparent reason.

Kavinnguaq remembered how, one winter, the camp folk had constructed an entire snow house for his parents' usage. Kavinnguaq had not been allowed to witness whatever had occurred therein, though the eerie orange glow of that overlarge *iglu*, illumed by lamp fire from within, had been etched into his memory. He remembered, too, how the glow had of a sudden winked out, to the accompaniment of adult wails; how a few adults, normally the strongest and surest of folk, had fled the place, bronzed faces drawn and panicked. Kavinnguaq had wondered, then, if he too should share in the fear, though the emotion had simply not arisen in his breast. Weirdness had always followed in his parents' wake, and he felt a mischievous sort of affection for both of them whenever their ways unsettled others.

Afterward, the camp folk had loaded Kavinnguaq's arms with massive cuts of frozen meat—to the point where Kavinnguaq's pre-adolescent arms had failed, the meat falling across his caribou hide boots, and bruising his toes. Kavinnguaq was always the one who received these "gifts" for his parents; these and other things, like seal oil for his mother's lamp, or the best sorts of hides for clothing, or tools carved with finest precision. He supposed, sometimes, that his parents were sort of lazy, though they always seemed so busy, at home, with their little rituals and observances.

Kavinnguaq rarely received a gift meant for himself, and then only from his mother. So it was a special day when he got his little drum-shaped amulet. It was a present from his father—who seemed to hate that very term, "father." It was not that he tended toward unkindness to Kavinnguaq, but simply that he was cranky and a stickler for exactitude. Rather than using *ataata* (father), he favoured the term *ataataqsaq* (material for fatherhood) in describing his relationship to Kavinnguaq. Kavinnguaq's mother had ever frowned at this, preferring to simply term herself *anaana* (mother).

Unbeknownst to either parent, Kavinnguaq was unruffled by any chosen term. He knew that he had been adopted, for the aged couple whom he now thought of as parents had often explained that to him. Apparently, Kavinnguaq's birth parents had been killed before his ability to retain such an event in memory. They had not been from this camp. And they had been slain by something very bad, something too frightening for even his adopted Angakkuq parents to talk about. It was that event, his current parents claimed, that had stolen Kavinnguaq's voice and true name away from him. No one would ever know other than Kavinnguaq's new name (Ear-drum), nor would Kavinnguaq have ever been able to utter it, had he remembered.

Wordless as ever, Kavinnguaq merely smiled when presented with his amulet. It held special significance, he knew, because his adopted father had been renowned for his drum-dancing. Once, the old man had been able to ripple the very air with his low and liquid songs, the rhythmic stepping that accompanied each stroke of the drum's edge. His peculiar Strength had seemed to tug at unseen things, writhing at the edges of one's vision, from some Hidden sleeve within the very air; though the elder, Kavinnguaq knew, would never again hold a drum in hand.

Perhaps it was his father's eyes, unfocused and rheumy, that made Kavinnguaq know. Perhaps it was the effort with which the man rose even up onto an elbow from his sleeping pallet. Perhaps it was the caribou hides, piled high over his attenuated frame, in an attempt to block out an ever-present chill. Perhaps it was the way in which Kavinnguaq's mother spoke slowly to the old man, sadly, with a special respect that was not ordinarily there.

Or, perhaps, it was simply that Kavinnguaq knew because he knew; because there was a tongue within him, unexplained and unabashed, that spoke silent truth whenever a thing of great import occurred.

He *knew* that his adopted father—to Kavinnguaq, his only father—was about to die.

Kavinnguaq's mother knew it, too. He could sense that, as well, even without the sight of her frightful eyes, her strained features. And for the first time in his life, Kavinnguaq felt some urge to speak, some need for sound, pushing up from his insides. But he could do nothing other than absorb her sadness, her utter devastation, through his eyes. He could do nothing other than lean close to his father, clutching the drum amulet in hand. With his own nostril against his father's, cheek against cheek, he snuffled out a sort of kiss.

"You should leave, now, Kavinnguaq," the boy's mother told him, her eyes yet upon her husband. One fluid line sped down from eye to chin, a tear like fast and sudden rain.

Kavinnguaq made no motion to depart, his vision flickering back and forth between his parents. His father smiled, then, issuing a weak and somehow wet chuckle.

"I'll call you when it's all right, Kavinnguaq," his mother

added. "There are things you're not ready to see, yet."

The old man's smile fell at her words. "No, wife," he told Kavinnguaq's mother. "We agreed. He can never be an Angak-kuq. That which holds his voice makes it too dangerous." He took a moment to cough, before adding, "How can he voice the *irinaliutit*? When will he sing the *sakajjuiit*? There is no being an Angakkuq without voice."

Kavinnguaq's mother was silent for a long moment, after which she muttered:

"There is something of the Some Seen to him. He should be taught. He should follow in your knowledge, husband."

"That which stole his name, his voice, still has them," Kavinnguaq's father argued. "Makes it too dangerous. If you do not do things the natural way, it could reverse the Strength of the Land. Render it *kiglurittuq* (backwards)."

The tears of Kavinnguaq's mother ran freely, then. She fell silent again, for some minutes. When she at last spoke, the sound from her voice was like the sough of chill wind:

"Then I lose everything, husband."

"You do not lose me," the old man insisted. "Remember your own knowledge, wife. Don't make this darkness to catch you up. It isn't real, unless you agree with it."

Yet Kavinnguaq's mother only muttered to herself, as though she hadn't heard. As the boy leaned closer to her, in concern, he saw her reach one hand toward the other. There, she removed the two ivory rings she'd always worn side-by-side, one on the middle finger, another on the adjacent ring finger. In a weary sort of gesture, she cast these before Kavinnguaq's father, who hissed in alarm.

Then Kavinnguaq heard his mother's voice, which arrived like a guttering flame:

"I am broken, now. And alone. My heart has become a vessel of tears. And this is the last truth I can ever speak."

Even as his mother uttered the statement, Kavinnguaq

could feel the Strength within her, like some great dome that had cracked, pulling all of its mass inward with a living surge; and he watched as her small frame shivered violently. Kavinnguaq's own body became locked in place upon sensing even the merest edge of her inner storm: he wanted to shuffle away from her, as though to avoid a wash of frigid tide across his flesh; at once, he wanted to embrace her, to pull his mother away from some black swell beyond all but terror's understanding.

Of his parents, Kavinnguaq best cherished his mother. Though he had not the least of grips upon whatever was now transpiring, its simple echo left a part of his being raw, like a lesion born of the whip across bare skin.

"Go, Kavinnguaq," the boy's father said. The dying man's voice was damp, like the flap of water-swollen hide. His eyes were wide, of a sudden fearful, riveted upon the tear-streaked face of his wife.

The old man reached for the hand of his wife, whispering: "These feelings . . . dangerous . . ."

But his wife would not take his hand.

Kavinnguaq hesitated, quivering with indecision—then he rose and bolted out of his parents' tent. He stood for a moment, by the tent's opening, gulping mouthfuls of fresh outside air, making no attempt to process whatever dread thing he'd felt unfolding. He was nevertheless dogged by the feeling that he had witnessed a birth, of a sort, albeit that of something backwards and twisted. His mother had chosen a path. By some means it would not explain, his strange inner mind knew that.

He could not recall ever having felt lost or abandoned. But that was how he now felt. He tried to control his shaking.

Camp folk, a few adults, passed by, casting quizzical looks at Kavinnguaq. All, however, knew that he could not speak, just as all understood that there was no comprehending the doings of his family. One or two of the adults forced out smiles for the boy, though their eyes were full of trepidation. Kavinnguaq made no attempt to smile in return, any more than he might have smiled for dogs.

His eyes were drawn, instead, to the florid purple of the hillsides rising about the camp.

As Kavinnguaq watched, the brilliant sun of the month of Akullit died, covered over by a creeping shadow. A deep and all-encompassing mass of cloud, some gigantesque blanket rolled in ash or soot, came to close like a vast lid over the dome of the sky. Kavinnguaq watched its shadow move, akin to a stalking thing, over the hills, as though its darkness were devouring every flower; every boulder and blade of sedge; every rock and ridge. Two ravens, perched nearby and perhaps eyeing the camp for some evidence of scraps, shuffled uneasily beneath the expanding shade, before flying off.

All in the camp now stood in that shadow. Every face was upturned toward the dark cloud that had swallowed their world.

Adults gasped, muttered a bit, before a dread quiet reigned. Children ceased to play, some features threatening tears. Kavinnguaq could hear the dogs at the edge of the community, issuing brief yips and howls before joining in the great silence.

Then Kavinnguaq's father died. He could feel it. Just as he could feel something terrible enter into the community. Though he was no Angakkuq, he knew.

Kavinnguaq fled, then, speeding out of the community and into the hills.

Near mindless, chilled by the sweat that seemed to wring itself from every part of his flesh, he ascended the highest ridge he could find—then another, and another, until the camp was out of sight. All the while, his breath rasped in his throat, and his eyes sought out every horizon, looking for any distant part of the sky that might have remained free of cloud. Instead, there was not a bit of it that showed anything of the sun's light, and all points of the great Land seemed to recede into a night more akin to that of winter's reign.

Kavinnguaq's panic drove him, thereafter, to hide under a high, triangular boulder that had fallen to lie balanced upon two others. Kavinnguaq at last wept therein, not exactly understanding what he wept for; but only that the tears seemed to wash something poisonous from his core. Time became strange, as though days might pass with the ease of heartbeats; and the more natural darkness afforded by his shelter at last calmed him.

When Kavinnguaq emerged, a glance at the sky above, lightless and enduring, left him nauseated. He stood in the wind for a moment, dried tears leaving a crusty feeling across his cheeks, until he got his bearings.

He descended, after shuffling his way back to the community, into a camp where few people walked in the open. Those children who saw Kavinnguaq shied away from him (though it meant nothing, for Kavinnguaq had never been one for peers or play). Those adults who espied him cast strange, haunted looks in Kavinnguaq's direction, and some muttered as though in concern. One old woman hooked an arm around Kavinnguaq as he passed her, stopping him in a half-hug. She cooed with pity, and another woman stepped forward to join her, so that Kavinnguaq of a sudden knew:

He had been right. His father had died. The camp had found out about it.

Kavinnguaq turned his face up toward the women, feeling numb but not ungrateful, and wishing they would let him go. When they at last did so, he made his way back to his parents' tent, face down-turned.

He wanted only the embrace of his mother.

Kavinnguaq's mother was not present when he entered the tent. Her *qulliq*, the sort of soapstone lamp each adult woman owned, had been left unattended, and the cotton wads along its rim had been allowed to burn too low. Denied seal oil, they had gone out, plunging the tent into a deeper darkness than Kavinnguaq had ever known with open eyes. And it occurred to him, only then, that he had been gone for some time. He was extremely hungry, and he fumbled about until he found several helpings of *pipsi*—cross-cut fillets of dried char salmon—which silenced his stomach. As he chewed, his eyes adjusted to the dark. He stared at his father's empty sleeping pallet, and wondered who had removed the body from the tent. His mother had some male cousins in this camp. Perhaps they had done it.

Kavinnguaq cried a bit more, after that, before falling asleep. He had never actually witnessed those customs that prevailed, among adults, in the event of a death. But his imagination, it seemed, was bent upon recreating them from description. His dreams were filled with sombre song, with wailing at once Human and canine; with images of bodies wrapped round with hide, until they became no more than moth cocoons; piled high with rocks, until the very Land snatched them into itself, like some stone-toothed maw.

When Kavinnguaq awoke, the tent was still empty. His mother had not yet returned. Wringing the sleep from his eyes, he did not so much leave the dwelling as wander out of it, looking about the community for any sign of his mother or her relatives. There were few people about, yet again smiling in that shy way of theirs as they worked at this or that. Kavinnguaq did his best to be polite, moving away from them and toward the edge of the camp. There, he espied a number of moving figures, and became convinced, after a moment of staring, that they were just arriving into the community after having stepped out of it for a time.

A funeral cortege.

So they had removed his father, the most important part of whom perhaps now dwelt in that place he'd always spoken of: a better Land, where hunting was good, pain absent, and existence easy. But that meant, Kavinnguaq knew, that his father's lifeless frame lay enwrapped along with his personal amulets, protected from scavengers under a pile of stones. Kavinnguaq was happy at the idea of his father now living in comfort; though the thought did nothing to keep him from missing the man. Kavinnguaq swallowed with the force of a mute sob.

Kavinnguaq began to run toward his mother, whom he saw walking amidst those returning to the community. He made it three quarters of the way to her, before he stopped, staring.

There was something strange about his mother.

She stood erect, walking slowly, while her closest relatives walked behind and at her sides. One of her cousins even bent near her as they walked, whispering something that was as yet beyond earshot. Kavinnguaq's mother seemed not to answer, only staring ahead, expression akin to some visage carven in antler. And Kavinnguaq was struck by how her features bore no sign of her earlier grief.

Yet it was not her face that most concerned Kavinnguaq. It was her throat.

Fleetingly, Kavinnguaq wondered if his mother wore some strange article of clothing about her neck. But he quickly saw that such was not the case: instead, much of her neck—and her throat entire—was gripped round with a swollen clot of shade. This was not an object, so much as a place where the light was not; for it was devoid of texture or detail. It possessed boundaries, but only as a shadow might be delineated by the shape of whatever object had cast it. Kavinnguaq, however, could not imagine any kind of thing that might own such a silhouette, for he did not recognize its shape. As the people in the cortege brushed past him, some gripping his shoulder in sympathy, he struggled to view his mother more clearly.

At last, Kavinnguaq came to position himself directly in his mother's path.

She did not seem to see him, merely brushing past. As she did so, Kavinnguaq could hear several of her relatives speaking at her. Yet she stared ever ahead, seemingly emotionless, her lips never parting for reply. The relatives, also, soon fell silent.

"She's just in shock," came a male voice. Kavinnguaq

wheeled to see that one of his mother's cousins, trailing behind the cortege, had stopped to address him. "She still loves you," he added. "She just can't speak right now. It's how people are, sometimes, when they grieve."

But Kavinnguaq, using facial expression to the best of his ability, indicated that he did not agree. He placed a hand at his own throat, indicating the clot of shadow that seemed to ride around his mother's neck.

"She's not mad at you," the cousin said, giving Kavinnguaq's shoulder a squeeze. "She'll talk to you once she rests a bit."

Obviously, the man had not understood, and Kavinnguaq began to wonder: was it possible that he had not seen the shadowy thing?

His mother's cousin stepped around him, and Kavinnguaq stared after the cortege, studying their body language. Not one of the camp folk seemed taken aback by the appearance of Kavinnguaq's mother. Not one leaned away from her, or seemed to mutter fearfully amongst the others, or seemed to even badger as to what might be afflicting her. Yet Kavinnguaq himself had easily espied the throat-shade, even from afar.

Had no one else seen it?

Kavinnguaq shuddered, then, filled with a crawling strangeness at the thought, as well as at the thought of the expression his parents had so often used with one another:

"Some Seen."

Leaden with dread, Kavinnguaq made his way back to his tent, into which his mother and three of her cousins had disappeared. He stood outside of the tent, making no attempt to mask how forlorn, how lost and confused, he now felt. A great deal of time went by, until the cousins, two men and a woman, emerged. They all, upon noticing Kavinnguaq, forced weak smiles to their faces.

"Don't be upset if she doesn't talk," one of the men said.

"Try to comfort her," added the woman.

Each gave Kavinnguaq a hug, before going to their own tents. Even after they'd departed, Kavinnguaq stood for a time. He found that he did not want to enter the tent. He felt something, like the essence of winter wind made into an emotion; and it seemed, now, to suck at all light and warmth from its centre, that tent. Somehow, Kavinnguaq had gone from wanting nothing other than his mother, to wanting anything other than her.

Still, in time, people came to stare at him, until the force of their gazes felt like coals across Kavinnguaq's skin. Eventually, in order to escape the camp's scrutiny, Kavinnguaq entered the tent.

It was as dark as before. Not needing vision to find it in the tiny confines of the dwelling, Kavinnguaq took his traditional place therein. But he was startled, as his eyes adjusted, to see the form of his mother. She knelt in the dark, face turned toward the tent's opening, and never in Kavinnguaq's direction. It took Kavinnguaq a moment to realize it, but he eventually noted that she did not kneel in her traditional spot. She knelt in the centre of her husband's sleeping pallet.

Kavinnguaq realized, then, that he feared her, though he did not know why. Had he possessed a voice, he still would not have called out to her. Of a sudden, he was glad of the fact that she did not seem to notice him.

Kavinnguaq adjusted his seating, shuffling in order to be a bit farther away from his mother, when he felt something hard at the edge of his hand. He grasped at it, realizing that it was his little drum amulet. Kavinnguaq had dropped it, earlier, upon falling asleep, and had forgotten to recover it upon waking. It was good, somehow comforting, to feel it in hand.

As Kavinnguaq's fingers closed around the amulet, there was a sharp intake of breath from his mother. Dimly, he could see the shape of her face as it turned in darkness, turned until it was directed at Kavinnguaq himself. Kavinnguaq could see, then, a deeper darkness as her mouth opened wide, issuing a sound like growl and croak admixed—a sound that prickled at the boy's entire skin, as he had never before heard such a noise, much less imagined it as a production of the Human throat.

Then Kavinnguaq shivered, for two points of light, like the merest sparks, shone from his mother's mouth. They were like eyes peering from some cave opening, and an inner part of Kavinnguaq, a secret part which had never before thought of being seen, somehow knew that it was being scrutinized.

Kavinnguaq then watched his mother's form bend forward, dipping low to the floor of the tent. On all fours, like some slow and slithering creature, she began to move through the darkness.

Dropping his amulet, Kavinnguaq fled.

○ ○ ○

The next few days were but the purest pall of horror for Kavinnguaq. He dwelt like some elusive spectre about the camp, occasionally dipping into tents to take food whenever hunger impelled him. He knew that people were talking about him, talking about his mother's strange behaviour, though he had no idea how to ask for help. Had he owned a voice, how would he have explained what only he could see? He had little grasp of it himself. Even in those moments when he sat far from camp, mastering his terror and self-pity long enough to contemplate it all, his thoughts led him only in circles.

Only a word in the specialized terminology of his parents kept coming to him: *ilummiqtaujuq*. It was a word, or so Kavinnguaq had gathered, for one in the grip of a bale thing. And that was how he now thought of his mother. She was ilummiqtaujuq. She had been taken, taken by . . . something, perhaps even given herself to it. One way or another, the being which now wore his mother like fine new winter clothes was not his mother. It was alive, thinking with inky thought, feeling with oily sentiment. Kavinnguaq sensed that much. Yet it was not her.

It was on Kavinnguaq's third miserable day that he again saw his mother—her body, at least—walking about the community. As ever, she stared ahead, as though fixed on a point far distant; and her steps were slow, measured, like those of a sleepwalker. Other people, Kavinnguaq noticed, had begun to avoid her, to make fearful faces as she passed. The other adults were not fools, and they could guess that something was wrong. Yet they were as powerless as Kavinnguaq himself. Who were they to go to? The camp's only two specialists in matters eldritch and dread, were gone. One Angakkuq had fallen by age and sickness. The other Angakkuq, the victim herself, had fallen by something far less natural.

It was while studying the reactions of the camp folk that Kavinnguaq first got a good look at the Clutcher. At least, that was how Kavinnguaq had come to think of it. In his mind, the thing that rode his mother's throat, that had perhaps even stared at him from her open mouth, was the *Tigummijuq* (That which Grabs).

Even with the heavy murk, a false twilight enforced by the clouds that had not departed since the death of Kavinnguaq's father, his mother threw a shadow. At best, there was not enough light for any normal camp dweller, Kavinnguaq included, to cast other than the merest of shades. Yet Kavinnguaq's mother *always* cast a shadow, deep and long, and as black as that which rode upon her throat. Kavinnguaq did not know what to make of it, any more than he knew what conclusion to draw from a single event he'd thus far witnessed. But he noted it from where he peered around the edge of a tent, trying not to be seen by the Clutcher. And he stored the fact away, in case the future might render it useful. He still wept from time to time, but having some facts on the Tigummijuq somehow allowed him to pretend that things could work out all right, and he clung to any illusion of control he might scavenge.

∘ ∘ ∘

All illusions, however, were dispelled on Kavinnguaq's fifth miserable day. He was again peering from around the edge of a tent, chewing, his cheeks filled like a lemming with *mipku*—some dried caribou that he'd pilfered—when one of his mother's cousins startled him by brushing past. At first, Kavinnguaq jumped, drawing back from the man, for the boy had become near feral in the last few days, having no interest in any foolish statements adults might aim at him.

Yet he was rooted with terror when he glanced upward and saw the man's neck.

There, covering the cousin's entire throat, rode a Clutcher. The Tigummijuq was exactly alike to that which rode Kavinnguaq's mother. Kavinnguaq could see its central mass, like some ebon mite, some parasite engorged with blackest blood, as well as four arms or legs encircling the neck. The thing was tucked well up under the chin, with no actual head in view.

Kavinnguaq afforded himself no further chance to gawk at the abomination. Some vast shudder seemed to run through his slight frame, before his legs took action. Together, they carried him away at best speed.

When Kavinnguaq was at last alone, heaving lungs slowing a bit, he tried to think matters out. As usual, rational thought failed him. He still had no idea what the Clutchers represented. He knew only that he was more terrified, more despairing, than ever before—for he'd never imagined that the things might spread. How many more of them would he find over the next few days?

Kavinnguaq's answer came in a matter of hours, as soon as he retuned to the community. The man who had brushed past him was not the only one to have gained a Tigummijuq. As Kavinnguaq roamed the camp, he found two more Clutchers: one upon his mother's other male cousin, the other upon her female cousin. As with Kavinnguaq's mother, all now moved like sleepwalkers, their eyes unfocused, as though heeding some voice at whisper for their ears alone.

Fortunately, they ignored all of the normal camp folk, including Kavinnguaq himself, who no longer felt compelled to hide from his mother. They walked in strange, overlapping circles, inflicting terror in their wake. Kavinnguaq noted that, while the camp folk could not see those things gripping their victims' throats, the normal folk nevertheless feared the madness that such weird behaviour seemed to denote. All laughter had died in the community; all play; all open conversation; all emotions other than terror.

○ ○ ○

On Kavinnguaq's seventh miserable day, he awoke under his sheltering rock, in his place among the hills. He was chilled, despite the many blankets he'd stolen, and his ear hurt where it had rested on a tiny chip of stone that had somehow managed its way into his bed. He had liberated a number of supplies, by now, from various tents. The adults—those normal ones who remained, anyway—all knew about it, and allowed him to do so. But he wondered what he would eventually do for food.

As had become his habit, Kavinnguaq steeled himself for one of his thrice daily checks on the community. Though there were now more Clutchers than normal folk, he was no longer frightened when he saw them—not even the walker children, whose tiny, circling bodies seemed particularly lurid. None of the walkers seemed truly aware. None seemed to register anything other than the strange, silent voice they heeded (or, at least, that was how it seemed in looking at them), and, while Kavinnguaq yet sensed a sort of deep malevolence in the abominations, he had not experienced a Clutcher's hostility since that day he'd witnessed his mother slithering in the tent.

No, they were now worse than frightening. For the sight of

them—especially his mother, whose beautiful silver hair had come loose to fly halfway over her face—ever pierced Kavinnguaq's heart with sorrow.

Kavinnguaq could see them even as he approached the camp: individuals of every age with exact and identical stepping; those rigid postures; the overlapping, circular paths. Then, as he got within a good stone's throw, he could see the darkness about all their throats. But there was today something else, some further strangeness, that seized Kavinnguaq's attention. It now seemed that the hands of the walkers had also become dark, though not in the same way as their throats. Every hand, every lower arm in the camp, seemed . . . reddish.

As Kavinnguaq approached, eventually coming to stand among the unheeding Clutchers, his skin came to crawl with the realization that he was seeing blood. From elbows to tips of fingers, the walkers were imbrued with life fluid. On a few, including his mother, the stuff lay caked across the front of caribou hide garments. Some, especially the children, showed red-flecked faces.

Yet Kavinnguaq could see no wounds.

It was some time later that Kavinnguaq found the source of the blood. With their bare hands, it seemed, they had killed the dogs.

Kavinnguaq had no idea how or why it had happened, but he found the bodies on the far side of camp—or, at least, those parts that had been rendered from them, for the dogs had been pulled to shreds. Kavinnguaq guessed, from the amount of meat and fur lying amid gore-splashed rocks, that not quite half of the dogs had fallen, while the rest had fled. In what was left of Kavinnguaq's tattered heart, he wished the survivors well.

He glanced at the sky, still like a mat of soot over his head. Not even the ravens wanted to eat under it. Not even the gulls. Nor a single fly.

On his way back into camp, Kavinnguaq spotted tent rings. They were circles of stones that had been used to pin down the sides of three separate family abodes. It was then that he knew: there were no longer any normal people in the camp. At some point, while Kavinnguaq had been sleeping or thinking or weeping, or simply lying numb out among the hills, the remaining few folk had decamped and fled. Kavinnguaq almost smiled at the thought. He harboured no ill sentiment over the fact that they hadn't asked him along.

After all, he had only one remaining family member. How could he simply leave her here?

∘ ∘ ∘

It was on Kavinnguaq's ninth miserable day that he heard them singing. It was what awakened him from the grip of ordinary nightmare. He could hear them, shrill and piercing, from all the way out among the hills.

Yet it was the sky that stilled the breath in his throat.

The clouds had shifted to a dark sanguine hue, as of aging blood—not quite as far as the eye could see, but in a vast zone around the camp.

When Kavinnguaq arrived, he could see every walker man, walker woman, and walker child in the camp. There were even a couple of toddlers, standing straight, as though held up by cords. Each Clutcher, it seemed, had moved its hostage body into the centre of the camp. Kavinnguaq could see his mother among them, the blood across her hands now dried and flaking in the wind. She, like all others, now stood, facing the coast, visage upturned to the sky. And all mouths were open in a terrible song. This was like a long whine admixed with a low hum, as though disparate voices struggled in each distinct throat. There were no actual words, but amid the discordant sounds there arose a warbling overtone, like a master voice wrought of many. It was like listening to some alien instrument, to an eldritch call, and it educed a feeling in Kavinnguaq's guts that brought his heart to speed.

As Kavinnguaq watched, bulbous growths extended themselves from every upturned mouth, though the singing went on without disruption. At first, Kavinnguaq thought that the growths were like tongues, however black as the Clutchers themselves.

It was the shadows that showed them for what they really were: every walker, like Kavinnguaq's own mother, cast a shadow long and grotesque, despite the louring sky. But the shadows were, of a sudden, different. Wherever Kavinnguaq's eyes rested on any shadow, wherever the figure's throat might be, he could *see* a Tigummijuq. The Clutchers, it seemed, did not cast shadows along with those they rode—but instead cast images of their true selves. Inside the shadows of all walkers, including Kavinnguaq's mother, he could see fleshy beings instead of inky clots. They were like skinned squirrels, their flesh mottled with the purple of old bruises, with the yellow-green of phlegm. Only in the shadows of their walkers could Kavinnguaq see the truth of the things—such as the fact that their heads, hairless and grinning and foetal, protruded like tongues from their victims' mouths. Their eyes were like tiny chips of quartz, and shone with a manic radiance, reminding Kavinnguaq of when his mother's Clutcher had regarded him, back in the tent, through her open mouth.

At the moment, the Clutchers seemed blind to Kavinnguaq, despite his now-close proximity. Together they remained focused on something above them. To it alone, they seemed to call.

Then something winked over Kavinnguaq's head.

Something had moved. And Kavinnguaq's vision flew upward, to wherever the Clutchers directed their song.

Had Kavinnguaq owned a voice, he would have cried out, then, for the sky over the camp seemed to roil with great eyes; with orbs that seemed to jostle and shift, like the sense organs of a thousand giants set to boil in red broth. Their irises were of all colours—with but a few gazing downward, while most simply rolled, as in madness. Some winked with lids of purest ebon, like one who has awakened from deep slumber, and now tries to get one's bearings. As Kavinnguaq beheld them, his own gaze wide and unblinking, he had the sense that he was not looking at manifold regards, but only one. These eyes, even the Clutchers themselves, belonged to a single, central vitality; perhaps a very old mind, whose workings were so strange that they seemed like the inverse of true thought. It was purest discord, Kavinnguaq's inner tongue, the secret one, told him, and mindless need.

The insight was too much for Kavinnguaq, who ducked into the nearest tent, fighting to breathe against a wrenching tightness in his chest. In sheer fright, rather than his usual sorrow, his eyes began to well. This was the thing, he guessed, of which his adopted parents had spoken. It was the life they would not name—that which had stolen away Kavinnguaq's birth parents, his voice, his original name. Had it always been here? Had it followed Kavinnguaq after the death of his birth parents? Had his adopted parents found it amusing to tease him with allusions to it, knowing all the while that it would one day seek him out?

Once Kavinnguaq became calmer, he dismissed such panic-spawned thoughts. In actual fact, he had no idea what the entity in the clouds signified. He knew not why the Clutchers sang to it, any more than he understood what the Clutchers themselves were. His mind at last ceased to reject that most awful truth of all: that there was no meaning in the Hidden parts of the Land, no sense to this Some Seen in which his parents had immersed themselves. To live was to know horror, and the Land promised order to Human life no more than landfall to a sea-tossed seed.

After some time, blessed numbness arrived. Huddled in the dark of the tent, Kavinnguaq heard the song stop. It took him a bit of time after that to realize that he was in his own tent—or, at least, the tent that had belonged to his parents. He knew it as soon as he shifted a knee, nearly breaking one of his adopted mother's ivory rings under it: one of her amulets, discarded in the madness of grief. Its twin was there, also, still intact, and Kavinnguaq held the rings in hand for a moment, enjoying their smoothness in his palm. Holding the objects led him to recall, within seconds, that he had left his own amulet nearby. When his mother's behaviour had earlier horrified him, he'd simply dropped the little drum-shaped carving.

Some groping about soon led him to his amulet, which felt strange together in hand with his mother's rings. As Kavinnguaq's father had carved the amulet, gripping it and the rings seemed a bit like holding his parents in miniature. He could almost feel their Strength, as though bound with invincible sinew to the articles of their faith.

Taking the amulets with him, Kavinnguaq left the tent, almost hesitating to glance at the sky, lest he again know the stare of those multitudinous orbs. He didn't get a chance to look at the sky, for his attention was caught by the sight before him, at ground level.

The walkers had finally turned their attention to him. All, his mother included, stood with shining eyes fixed upon Kavinnguaq's emergence. Their mouths hung open, seemingly stuffed with blackness, in which twin pinholes shone like minute eyes. These, Kavinnguaq knew, were the mirror images of the Clutchers themselves, staring at him. Kavinnguaq's skin, of a sudden, felt rimed with ice, breath suspended as he checked against the shadows thrown by the walkers. In all their cast shadows, the Clutchers seemed to squirm and shift, mottled flesh rippling. At the level of the shadows' mouths, tiny heads grinned up at Kavinnguaq, eyes aglow like so many sparks. The mouth of a given victim's shadow, he realized, was the true home to a Clutcher. By some facet of attainted Strength, it was a Clutcher's shade that one saw around a living neck, while the creature's actual substance thrived only in its victim's shadow. It was as though the creatures were inverse life, mirror-things—so that what should have been flesh was shadow, and what should have been shadow was flesh.

As one, the walkers emitted that chilling, roaring whine that Kavinnguaq had earlier heard from his mother. Then each

child, woman, and man slid in a strangely boneless fashion to the ground, until they were on all fours, abdomens nearly brushing the ground. Crawling in this way, with long and fluid movements, eyes unblinking and fixed upon Kavinnguaq, they neared him in a half-circle.

The amulets, Kavinnguaq realized: they came after him whenever he held as much as one amulet.

As though dropping embers, Kavinnguaq let go of the amulets, so that they bounced from the toes of his boots to scatter in dust. His mother, he'd remembered, had already behaved this way upon recovery of his little carven drum. The Clutchers, by whatever fell vibrancy impelled them, seemed to detest such items of Strength. If Kavinnguaq were to survive, he would have to make sure that he treated the amulets like the embodiment of plague.

Sure enough, the walkers ceased to stalk. With that strange coordination that seemed to govern them, they collectively gained their footing once again. They stared, along with the shadow-eyes of the Clutchers in their mouths, for only moment longer. All were still, but for their dishevelled hair, whipped in the wind. All was silent, but for the heart that seemed to thunder in Kavinnguaq's own throat.

Then the eyes of the walkers again became fey, distant, and all returned to that walking, walking—walking in circle that overlapped circle.

Kavinnguaq turned his own face downward, watching one of his tears spatter across the tip of a boot. He was, he realized, more of a prisoner than any walker. In frustration, he even found himself wishing that a Tigummijuq had taken him.

Yet no such thing would ever happen, he sensed. He didn't have a voice, did he? He knew that they had not bothered to claim him for one simply reason: he'd have been unable to sing as one with them.

His eyes fell across the amulets, merely at the edge of his feet, yet utterly barred from his touch. For if he held them long enough, the walkers—even his own mother—would rend him as surely as if he'd been one more dog. His self-pity gave way, then, as did his grief; and a new emotion housed itself in his breast.

For the first time, Kavinnguaq felt *anger*. Not the familiar frustration at being denied knowledge, nor the sort of irritation he'd experienced over the foolishness of others, but a fury that seemed to stand upon an altogether new plane of being.

It was wrath. And it was redder than that nameless thing in the sky. More sanguine than the blood of the dogs.

The new emotion reigned in Kavinnguaq, flushing out all others, so that he stooped and picked up the amulets: the two rings of his mother—the only mother he'd ever known, and the drum carving of the only father he'd ever remember. He squeezed the three tight in hand, newly accepting of the consequences.

The consequences were immediate.

The walkers wheeled, jaws hanging, and they again descended into their collective creep. Kavinnguaq did not see their approach, for he shut his eyes, hearing only the ghastly noise of their Clutchers, a rising cacophony that seemed to rake at his ears as he was encircled.

And Kavinnguaq readied himself for death.

Some time passed, however, and the noises were all Kavinnguaq heard.

When he realized that no hands had yet fallen upon him, he opened his eyes, startled to see a ring of walkers nearer than arm's length from him, yet bobbing on all fours. He could see all the familiar faces of the camp folk: that of his mother; her two male cousins; her one female cousin; a child he had once tried playing with; even the old woman who had tried to comfort him upon the death of his father. Still, the eyes of Clutchers stared, spark-like, from their mouths. Still, their shadows held images of the true Clutchers, looking like skinned squirrels of piebald colouration.

Kavinnguaq waited, as did the Clutchers about him. Then,

it seemed, there came the barest hint of words admixed with the Tigummijuq din:

Spare us, Angakkuq . . .

Then Kavinnguaq reared his head to gaze at the multitude of eyes that roiled and winked above him. And it seemed that something in himself, a facet but Some Seen, exploded like light in his breast, and in his vision. The chorus of the Clutchers was, of a sudden, subsumed in the sweep of a new song: a thing at once like the touch of sun and water. And Kavinnguaq knew, then, that he had never lost his name; that his parents had merely spoken to him in the riddles of their kind. And with such understanding, he uttered his first word in living memory:

"Qilaut."

("Drum.")

It was his true name. And its Strength, held in reserve by some mystery of the Land, swept lightsome and right betwixt Land and Sky, shaking Kavinnguaq's frame like a vital charge. It shot through him, it seemed, so that its crown anchored itself in his vision, its tail resting in his parents' amulets. He rose up on his toes as he felt it, and his arms stretched wide.

The boy, now Qilaut, felt the Strength at voice in the well of his being, and he followed it. It first guided him to walk among the Clutchers. And everywhere he stepped, he placed a foot within some shadow. And as his foot touched a Tigummijuq, he whispered:

"Free yourself."

Wherever a foot fell, along with spoken word, it reversed that attainted Strength of which the Clutchers were made, so that they faded along with their gripping shadows. In the end, they had never been anything other than emotions—and dark ones, at that—wrought to resemble life. They returned, then, to the stuff of which they were made: invisible fears; reticence to embrace the vital swell; vision affixed to shadow instead of light; and desolation of the heart.

Yet guided by his Strength, Qilaut helped each victim to
his or her feet, brushing fingers across every individual throat. The
shadows were no longer there, but the eyes of the camp folk were
yet hazy and uncomprehending. Their eyes again filled with light
and personality, with every touch, and the utterance of:

"Awaken yourself."

Qilaut's mother was the last to awaken, and her eyes met
those of her son, of a sudden comprehending all that had transpired. At once, she fell to her knees, sobbing without shame or
hindrance—at last accepting the grief that had seized her Strength,
and turned her very selfdom into a lightless pit.

Many of the camp folk were similarly weeping, though
the swells of emotion around Qilaut, he sensed, were but healthy
ones. They were the terrible truths, the partially hidden sadness,
the wants or regret that all had pretended to bury for the sake of
workaday existence. They were the personal horrors, great and
small, that practical life could not allow to emerge. Such individual darknesses, he now knew, had eventually joined in a great
tide: a whirlpool of negative life which attainted Strength had
latched itself onto, like a hook drawing forth some monstrous
and deformed fish. Slowly, almost beyond all notice, it had drawn
the order of life toward a cycle that was withershins and bent.
Qilaut's senses, however, that inner tongue which now spoke to
him without whisper, told him that the camp folk had at last chosen correctly—had, in the end, chosen to allow his lead; to follow
his lamp from darkness. The order was now restored.

After some time, Qilaut assisted his mother to her feet. She
was smaller than he remembered, it seemed. She was no longer an
Angakkuq. His insight told him as much, so he did not offer her
the ivory rings; for her Strength, like that of his father, had poured
into himself.

"You've learned what an Angakkuq does," she said while
embracing him. "When one can no longer guide others from the
what is not to the *what is*, one can no longer be called an Angakkuq.

I will weep for you, my son, that my burden—and your father's—is passed to you. And I'll rejoice for the same."

The newly born Angakkuq, Qilaut, at last turned his face up toward the sky, and there were gasps of amazement at the fact that the mute boy now owned a voice. Frowning at the attainted whorl of Strength above him, he told it:

"There is no need for you, here, any longer. Remember, now, that you are made of nothing."

At once, the sky shifted, its sanguine giving way to soot. As one, the eyes above closed their ebon lids, receding back into the clouds. Qilaut reached out with his newly found *qaumaniq*, with the light of his Angakkuq Strength, to see if the thing was gone.

He found that it was so.

Then he collapsed against his mother, allowing her embrace to enfold him, as he wept bitter tears; for he was still a boy, and his mind was uneasy with those ideas his heart had accepted. He wept in relief, but also in mourning for the simple ignorance of his past self, Kavinnguaq, who had passed on as surely as his father.

"It's all right," his mother said, rocking him gently, "we all miss our darkness."